Alison Roberts is a New Zealander, currently lucky enough to be living in the South of France. She is also lucky enough to write for the Mills & Boon Medical Romance line. A primary school teacher in a former life, she is now a qualified paramedic. She loves to travel and dance, drink champagne, and spend time with her daughter and her friends.

MELTING THE TRAUMA DOC'S HEART

ALISON ROBERTS

MILLS & BOON

First published in Great Britain 2019
by Mills & Boon, an imprint of HarperCollins*Publishers*
1 London Bridge Street, London, SE1 9GF

Large Print edition 2020

© 2019 Alison Roberts

ISBN: 978-0-263-08551-8

CHAPTER ONE

OH, MAN...

He shouldn't have done that.

Isaac Cameron stared at the phone in his hand. He could hear the echoes of that angry edge in his own voice. Should he ring back and leave another voicemail to apologise? To admit that it was actually none of his business?

He thought about that for a moment as he tipped his head back and took a deep breath of the clean, crisp air around him. The snow-covered, craggy peaks of the mountains that bordered this small, Central Otago township in New Zealand caught his gaze and held it as he opened his eyes again. It hadn't got old yet, this view, despite the fact that he'd been living and working here for nearly a year. If anything, it had got into his blood.

And, okay, he might have come here as a last resort, to lie low and find out if there was anything left of the man he used to be, but it didn't feel like an escape any more.

He cared about this place. About the hardworking farming community that surrounded Cutler's Creek. About the small, rural hospital he worked in. About Don Donaldson—the man who'd kept this hospital up and running for decades, like his father before him, in the face of repeated threats of closure.

That was why he'd made that call.

And he wasn't going to call back and apologise. Because he wasn't sorry.

Because tapping back into the ability to care again was precisely the reason Isaac had come to this quiet corner of the world in the first place. Not to care too much, mind you, because he knew only too well how that could leave devastation and burn-out in its wake. But caring enough for something to really matter—like the situation that had prompted him to make that phone call—was part of what made a life meaningful, wasn't it? It was making Isaac feel human again. To hope, albeit cautiously, for a future that could provide contentment, if not happiness.

He slipped the phone into the pocket of the unbuttoned white coat he was wearing over his jeans and open-necked shirt. Would the woman he'd never met respond to that message? Did *she* care about any of the things that had become important to him in the last year? Probably not, so maybe it would do her good to hear what he had said. Everybody needed a wake-up call once in a while, didn't they? Like the one he'd had that had prompted him to apply for the rural hospital job he'd found advertised in a tiny country at the bottom of the world that he'd barely heard about.

The senior doctor and medical director of Cutler's Creek Hospital hadn't been that pleased to see him when he'd turned up, mind you.

'*You're over-qualified. Why the hell would we need a trauma surgeon with your kind of experience in a place like this? Why would you even want to live here? You'll be bored stiff.'*

'I'm over big cities and war zones. I need a break from patching people up when what's wrong with them wouldn't have happened if people could be a bit kinder to each other. I can do general medicine along with trauma. I've been in plenty of situations where there's been nobody but me to provide what's needed.'

Maybe it had been due to the remnants of that kind of autonomy that had prompted him to take matters into his own hands and make that regrettable phone call. Well, it was too late to worry about any repercussions now and it was time he headed back inside. There was a chill in the air that suggested the forecasters hadn't been wrong in predicting a storm that would usher in the first of the winter weather.

Isaac turned back towards the rambling, low-slung, wooden building that was Cutler's Creek Community Hospital. They had a ten-bed capacity here, including maternity and geriatrics, an outpatients' department, a main operating theatre that hadn't been used for years, and a smaller one that was used for minor procedures and as their equivalent of an emergency department where they could assess and deal with accidents and medical emergencies with resources like ultrasound, ECG, X-ray and ventilation equipment. It was by no means a large hospital but it was more than enough to keep two doctors busy as the medical hub for a community of several thousand people.

The man who had kept this hospital going—thriving even, given that the community had raised the funds for their new ultrasound equipment only recently—was walking towards Isaac as he headed back inside. Don Donaldson was scowling but that was nothing new. He'd been scowling just like this the first day Isaac had met him when he couldn't understand why he'd even applied for the job here. He knew a lot more about his boss now and, like everybody else, he accepted that this man's heart of gold was well covered by grumpiness that could border on being plain rude, but who could blame him, given the cards that life had already dealt? He'd never remarried after his wife had walked out on him decades ago, taking his only child with her to the other side of the globe. He'd come home to find his father was terminally ill and there was nothing he could do to help, had then devoted his life—often single-handedly—to giving Cutler's Creek a medical service to be proud of and now…

Well, now things might have just become a whole lot worse. It seemed that history was about to repeat itself.

'Zac… Good. You're still here.'

'I wasn't planning on heading home any time soon. I'm going to do another ward round while I'm waiting for Faye Morris to come in. Sounds like it's not a false alarm for her labour this time. Debbie's coming in with her so I'll just be available if she needs backup. Given her experience and skills as a midwife, I'll probably just be catching up on some reading.'

'Right...' The older man cleared his throat. 'Well, I just wanted to make sure you're not going to say anything. To anyone. You know how fast word gets around in a place this size and I do not want my mother upset—especially not now when she's got a big celebration coming up. This is nobody's business but mine and it's up to me who I tell. And when.'

Too late, Isaac thought. He lifted his gaze to the mountains to avoid eye contact that might reveal his discomfort over the fact that he'd already betrayed what he'd known was a confidence, even if it hadn't been stipulated as such at the time.

'I still don't agree with you, Don. You can't just diagnose yourself with something like pancreatic cancer and then give up. Have you even thought about a differential diagnosis? You wouldn't treat your patients like this so why do it to yourself?'

'Because I watched my own father do exactly what you think I should do. He went and got a formal diagnosis. He got persuaded to get the surgery, and chemo and radiation and, okay, maybe he got a few extra months from that but what good were they to anyone, especially him? He was mostly bedridden and suffering, dying by inches...' Don cleared his throat again but his voice still sounded raw, even after all these years. 'I'm not going like that, thanks very much. I've got unfinished business here and I intend to do whatever I can for as long as I can.'

'But you don't even know that you're right. Let me have a look at you and run a few tests. At the very least, let me do an ultrasound.'

'I've got exactly the same symptoms my dad had. You know as well as I do that inherited gene mutations can get passed from parent to child. That as many as ten percent of pancreatic cancers are genetic. Look... I just *know*, okay? I've known for quite a while now. I've been diagnosing illnesses for the best part of half a century. Are you trying to tell me I'm no good at my job?'

'Of course not.' Zac suppressed a sigh. 'And I'll support you in whatever way I can, you know that.'

He wasn't about to give up on this but he knew that continuing to push right now would only lead to Don shutting himself off completely. He was a private man and Zac could respect that better than most people, given that he was one himself.

'I just need to know that you'll keep this to yourself. I shouldn't have said anything. I wouldn't have, if you hadn't come barging into my office like that. Without the courtesy of even knocking...'

'Hmm...' A sideways glance showed him that Don was now the one avoiding eye contact and he understood why. He still felt uncomfortable that he'd seen too much. He'd be just as embarrassed as his boss if the tables had been turned.

'You caught me in a low moment, that's all it was. It won't happen again.'

A low moment? The man had been in tears. Trying to cover that up in the face of Zac's unexpected appearance, he had dropped the archive filing box that he had been stretching to replace on a high shelf. Despite being told to get out, Zac had automatically stooped to help pick up the contents of the box, which appeared to be a collection of unopened letters and parcels. *Not Known at This Address* and *Return to Sender* had been stamped all over them in red ink.

'Who's Olivia Donaldson?'

'Nobody. Just get out, Zac.'

'Not until you tell me what's going on. She's your daughter, isn't she?'

'Was...'

'She's dead?'

'As good as... We haven't had contact in more than twenty years. It doesn't matter now, anyway... Or it won't soon enough...'

The power of the internet meant that it had taken very little time to track down the woman who'd never opened those parcels or letters. A call to someone he knew in Auckland had given him access to a personal phone number. And, okay, he shouldn't have made that last call but what was done was done and it was highly unlikely that this Olivia Donaldson would take the slightest notice of what he'd said.

'Let's get back inside, Don. This wind feels like it's coming straight off the top of one of those mountains.'

'Yep...there's a storm brewing, all right.'

Isaac shook off the double meaning in those words that only he was aware of. It was a waste of energy to try crossing bridges before they were even visible. He had learned long ago to live in the present and deal with whatever came at you from left field. And he might be more than a bit of a lone wolf, but he was also definitely a survivor. He wasn't worried...

Stiletto heels made a very satisfying clicking sound on the gleaming floors of one of Auckland's most prestigious private hospitals. Along with the sleek, fitted skirt and matching jacket and the equally sleek hairstyle Olivia Donaldson had perfected long ago, she knew she looked the part of an up-and-coming plastic surgeon who was well on the way to being exactly where she wanted to be—at the top of the field in reconstructive microsurgery.

She'd had doubts about the value of providing cosmetic surgery to people who were wealthy enough to chase the illusion of perfection but she'd decided to view purely aesthetic surgery a stepping stone when she'd decided to apply for this job. Elective procedures like a facelift needed the same skills as reconstructive microsurgery and the hours and pay of this new job gave Olivia the freedom to do any further postgraduate study she would need.

Auckland's Plastic Surgery Institute had its own ward in this private hospital and Olivia's patients had had their surgery this morning. She had been pushed to get through all her cases today and they had all been breasts. A breast lift and augmentation for a mother of three in her forties, a breast lift and reduction for a woman in her fifties, and an implant removal for someone the same age as Olivia, who'd experienced hardened scar tissue from silicone material leaking from her implants. The lift and augmentation had been her first case this morning and Olivia could see no reason for her not to go home now.

'Sleep as upright as possible for the next forty-eight hours,' she advised. 'Prop your-self up on lots of pillows, or use a recliner chair if you've got one.'

'It hurts more than I expected.'

'We'll give you something for that but you can expect your breasts to be swollen and sore for the next few days, I'm afraid.'

'This instruction sheet says I have to avoid any strenuous activity for two to three weeks. That's not going to be easy when I've got three small children, is it?'

Olivia made an effort to keep her smile sympathetic. 'I'm sure it won't be, but it is very important. Especially not to lift them.

You'll risk tearing stitches and other problems if you do.'

At least her breast reduction patient was more thrilled with the new shape of her body beneath the support bandaging and surgical bra.

'I can't think why I didn't do this years ago. I just wish I'd got you to do a tummy tuck at the same time, Dr Donaldson.'

'We can talk about that another time. It wasn't a minor procedure that you had today, you know. How's the pain level now?'

'I've been too excited to notice it much. How soon can I go back to work and show it all off?'

'Once you no longer need your prescription pain medication. In a week or so, I expect, but we can let you know when you come for your first outpatient appointment at the Institute in a few days.'

'Will I be seeing you then?'

'Of course.' Olivia's smile felt slightly forced. A lot of her time these days was spent in the luxurious consultation rooms of the

Plastic Surgery Institute. Initial consultations to discuss desired procedures. Assessment and detailed planning in conjunction with the patients and then the follow-up appointments to track recovery and deal with any complications. And, even during the six months that Olivia had become immersed in the world of private cosmetic surgery, she was already seeing patients returning for their next procedure. It was flattering that they demanded to see her but it was a little disturbing, as well.

People getting addicted to cosmetic surgery in the hope of making their lives perfect was no myth and body dysmorphic disorder—where people became obsessed with a slight or even imagined defect in their appearance—was something Olivia intended to research more thoroughly in the near future.

The mental state of the last patient she checked on before discharging from the initial post-operative care was also a bit of a worry.

'I'm confident we managed to get all the scar tissue out,' Olivia assured her. 'You should find a dramatic improvement in any discomfort you were having after you recover from the surgery.'

Her patient was in tears. 'I can't look. I'm going to look worse than I did before I had the implants, aren't I? Nobody's going to want to even look at me. I'll be flat-chested again and now I'll have all these scars, as well. I can't believe I was stupid enough to do something like this in my twenties. Why does *anybody* do it?'

'Don't beat yourself up, Janie.' Olivia took extra time to try and reassure this patient and let her know that there were counselling services available through the Institute that she might find helpful. She was running a little late for her six o'clock appointment by the time she left.

'You're so lucky, you know,' Janie said by way of farewell. 'You're never going to need to even think of having any plastic surgery.'

It was walking distance from the hospital to

the Plastic Surgery Institute, which was one of many buildings devoted to private health care in this prestigious suburb of Auckland, some of which were converted mansions on either side of the tree-lined streets. Normally Olivia would have enjoyed the swirl of autumn leaves drifting down around her but she was trying to pinpoint why her day was feeling as if it had been somewhat unsatisfactory. The surgeries had all gone smoothly and theatre staff had been complimentary about her skills. She'd had plenty of practice in breast surgery during her training, though, and she'd taken great pride in doing the best job she could in breast reconstruction for women who'd had cancer surgery. Now that *had* been satisfying…

The waiting room of the Institute was full, which wasn't unusual. Any private clinic had to cater for clients who wanted an appointment after normal working hours. Olivia didn't have a clinic to run this evening, however.

'I'm just popping in for that six p.m. meeting,' she told the receptionist. 'I believe Simon wanted to see me?'

'He's waiting for you.'

Olivia couldn't miss the knowing hint in the look she was receiving. Had someone in the administrative staff started a rumour that something was going on between her and her boss? Maybe they all thought it was only a matter of time before something happened. She was single, after all, and who could resist the charms of one of the most eligible bachelors in Auckland's A-list society?

Olivia could, that's who. She held the receptionist's gaze until the young woman looked away, flushing slightly.

'Can you let him know his next client is here already?'

Simon's office had an enormous desk, leather chairs and a glass display case of antique surgical instruments.

'Sharon told me to tell you that your next client is here already.'

'She can wait for a minute or two. Oh, wait... I think it's a "he". Our new campaign to persuade men that aesthetic surgery is not just for women is starting to pay off. Literally...'

Olivia heard an echo of that slightly bitter compliment her last patient of the day had given her—that she was lucky that she wouldn't have to think about surgical enhancement of any kind. Simon was the male equivalent, wasn't he? Every feature perfectly symmetrical and his grooming and taste in clothes contributing to make him look years younger than forty-five. Even those grey streaks in that immaculate haircut could have been put there just to make him look more attractive.

As he stood up from his desk and put his jacket back on, she thought he looked as though he'd just stepped out of a magazine page—from an advertisement for luxury Italian suits, perhaps.

'So... Did you get my message?'

'Um...'

'You forgot to switch your phone back on after being in Theatre, didn't you?'

Olivia groaned. 'Sorry… It's been a long day. What was the message?'

'A last-minute invitation to a charity gala tomorrow night. The guest speaker is a London doctor who rang here this morning asking after you. He knew your mother well, he said, and he wanted to arrange a chance to pass on his personal condolences. He was out of the country on a sabbatical at the time of her funeral, he said, and by the time he got back, you'd already made the move here.'

Anybody who was anybody in London had known Olivia's mother, Janice, thanks to her position as one of the city's leading cardiologists and her thriving Harley Street practice. That spotlight had extended to Olivia, as her daughter, as well, bringing with it a pressure that had never felt comfortable. Escaping that spotlight was one of the reasons she had chosen to come back to New Zealand.

'I'm not sure, Simon.' Olivia knew she was frowning. 'I've never liked being in a crowd of people I don't know and any formal dresses I own are still in storage until I find an apartment I want to buy.'

'But you've got a day off tomorrow, haven't you? You could go shopping for a new dress. And this is how you get to know people. The important people.'

Attending functions like charity galas had been pretty much her mother's only social life. It had been at a charity event she had attended with her mother that she'd met Patrick, in fact—the man everybody, including herself, had expected her to marry. That breakup had been the other, even bigger reason she had decided to come back to the country of her birth to make a fresh start in her life. Olivia knew that her mother would have shrugged off the failed relationship as no more than an inconvenience. She also knew what she would have said about going to this event.

Go, Olivia. It's important to be seen. This is your career. The most important thing in your life. The only thing you can really count on…

'You don't have to go alone,' Simon added with an encouraging smile. 'I'll be there. I'll look after you, I promise.'

Olivia couldn't help glancing at the door as if looking for an escape route. Simon couldn't possibly know how much of a nerve he was stepping on. That he was reminding her of exactly how her relationship with Patrick had started—and its disastrous ending not that long after her mother's death—when he'd moved on to someone who offered an even better step up the social ladder.

Simon had followed her glance. 'You're right,' he said. 'I'd better get on with seeing my next patient.' He went to open the door for Olivia. 'Let me know what you decide. Maybe we can meet up for a drink before the event and that way you won't have to go in by yourself.'

Olivia fished her phone out of her pocket and turned it on as she left the building. It really was a very bad habit to turn her phone off but she knew that a staff member could easily find her if there was a problem on theatre days and she hated even the possibility of distractions when she was operating. Hearing the chime of an incoming message, she glanced at the screen, expecting it to be the message Simon had left about the invitation to the gala tomorrow, but it wasn't. It was a voicemail that had been left a couple of hours ago. From an unknown number.

Curious, Olivia keyed in her code as soon as she was sitting behind the wheel of her car, turning on the ignition as the message started to play.

'My name is Isaac Cameron,' a male voice said. There was a hint of an accent there. An Irish lilt, maybe? 'I'm a doctor at Cutler's Creek Hospital.'

Olivia gasped. Hearing the name of that small Central Otago township was disturbing, to say the least. She had a sudden urge to cut the call and delete the message but it was too late. She had been captured by the sound of the stranger's voice.

'I don't suppose you want to hear this,

Olivia Donaldson, but—you know what? I'm going to tell you anyway.'

She could hear the indrawn breath, as if the caller was about to start a lengthy story. And there was something about his tone that sent a shiver down Olivia's spine. Without thinking, she turned off the engine of her car and slowly leaned back into her seat, touching the speakerphone icon on the screen. She had no idea what this was about but it felt like it was going to be something significant. Potentially life-changing?

'I thought you should know that your father's dying,' the voice continued. 'He's got pancreatic cancer, which is what killed *his* father about twenty years ago. Not that that bothered you, from what I hear, seeing as you apparently refused to come to your grandfather's funeral.'

She could hear a judgemental note in his voice and that put her back up. *For heaven's sake*, Olivia thought, *I was only thirteen years old. I'd never even met my grandfather that I could remember. I hadn't seen my fa-*

ther since he'd walked out on his family.
Why would anyone think I was expected to
travel from the other side of the world to go
to a funeral for a stranger?

'I wouldn't have known anything about you,' Isaac was saying now, 'but I found your father crying over a box of old letters. And parcels. All the things that you'd sent back to him over the years without even bothering to open them.'

Olivia's jaw dropped. He was accusing her of something she knew nothing about. Letters? Parcels? She'd never seen anything from her father. He'd never even made a phone call. She could remember being in floods of tears that first Christmas after he'd gone and her mother trying to comfort her.

'I know it's difficult, Olivia, but you
wouldn't want to grow up in a place like Cut-
ler's Creek, believe me. I don't think there's
even a proper school there. My new job in
London is going to give us both the most
amazing opportunities, you just wait and

see. We can even think about getting you that pony you've always wanted.'

Did her mother know something about that mail? Had she thought that cutting any links Olivia had to a small country town would help her embrace a new life in a huge city? She could imagine her mother being that determined. Convincing herself that she was doing the best thing for her daughter, even.

She tuned back into the continuing voice-mail. 'He loves you. He wants the chance to tell you that before he dies. I have no idea how long he's got but I imagine it's not that long because he's refusing to seek treatment.'

Why would he do that? Olivia could feel the frown line between her eyes deepen. Pancreatic cancer could kill in a matter of weeks in some cases if nothing was done. Why didn't he want to fight? Did he not have people in his life who could persuade him it was worth fighting?

As if to answer her question, Isaac was talking at the same time. There was a rising note of something like anger behind his words now.

'You probably don't know and maybe you don't even care but there's a whole community here in Cutler's Creek that thinks a great deal of your father. He's a good man and I think it's a crying shame that you turned your back on him.'

'I *didn't*,' Olivia said, her tone shocking her with both its volume and the outrage it contained. 'It was totally the opposite...'

'Maybe the past shouldn't matter now,' Isaac said, and it almost felt as if they were having a real conversation. 'If the people around here knew about this, they'd move heaven and earth to grant any last wish he might have but your father doesn't want anyone to know and, anyway, there's only one person who can do that, and that's *you*. You could stop him dying with that regret on his mind.'

There was a long moment's silence, then, as if the speaker was taking a long breath. Trying to control his emotional outburst, perhaps? Yes…when he spoke again, it was at a much slower pace. In a much quieter tone.

'I don't know you, Dr Olivia Donaldson,' he said. 'And I'm not sure I'd want to know someone who could turn their back on someone who loves them that much but I thought you should know. Before it's too late. Because…because if you've inherited even a fraction of the compassion for others that your father has, you wouldn't want to refuse to give him the one thing that would mean so much to him.'

Olivia could hear a breath being released as a sigh. 'You never know…one day it might be *your* dying regret. That you never gave him a chance…'

The click told her the call was ended. Another voice was giving her the automatic options of saving, deleting or listening to the message again. Olivia simply turned her phone off and, for the longest time, she sat there without moving a muscle. She was stunned. Shaking, even.

It shouldn't matter this much. It was ancient history. Maybe she was just feeling angry that a stranger was blaming her so unfairly. Telling her that it was *her* behaviour that had caused someone grief. Enough grief that, after all these years—decades, in fact—this father that she hadn't seen since she was a young girl had been *crying*? She tried to shake off the unpleasant knot that was trying to form in her stomach. She didn't care about this man. She hated him, in fact. He'd walked out on her without a backward glance.

Or had he?

Was it true? About the mail? What had been in those parcels? Books, maybe. The thought slid into her head uninvited. Unwelcome. Her father had always given her books. He'd been the one to read the bedtime stories when she was too young to read for herself. She could remember the way he'd lounged on the edge of her bed, his elbow propped on her pillow so that she could snuggle into the crook of his arm as she listened.

Olivia closed her eyes tightly. She recognised that prickly sensation that was tears trying to form. She hadn't shed any tears over her father for longer than she could remember. But remembering him reading to her had unlocked so many things that she'd buried. There had been a time when she'd missed him *so* much... She'd missed his hugs, that gleam in his eye that told her he was proud of her, that rich chuckle that was his laughter and...and even his smell, which came from that old-fashioned aftershave he insisted on using.

That knot in her stomach was tightening enough to be painful. Olivia felt like she was being attacked on all sorts of emotional fronts. She'd only lost her mother a matter of months ago and she was going to become an orphan now? With no close family at all? There was a possibility that her mother had betrayed her long ago but even if that was the case, why hadn't her father tried harder? How unfair was it that he had given up and then blamed *her*? Okay, she had refused to go to her grandfather's funeral when her mother had passed on the information and message from her father and she had written a response telling him that she never wanted to hear from him again but she'd only been a teenager. A kid. He'd been the adult. If he'd really cared that much, he would have tried again.

And, on top of all that, here was this complete stranger judging her and deciding she wasn't a person worth knowing. It was so unfair that it couldn't be allowed to go unanswered. Olivia flicked her phone on. She was going to return that call and tell this Isaac Cameron exactly what she thought of someone who could attack someone they knew nothing about.

Maybe she would write another letter to her father as well and put things straight about who had turned their back on whom. Or…her finger was still a little shaky as she poised it over the icons on the screen of her phone…she could do it face to face. Like an adult instead of a petulant teenager. Because, if she did that, she'd know for sure what the truth actually was. And maybe she needed to know the truth.

The icon that she chose to press instead was a browser. Just to find out how hard it might be to get to Cutler's Creek. Dunedin was the nearest city but there was an airport in Queenstown, as well. With a rental car it wouldn't take too long to get deeper into the centre of the South Island. If she left early enough, she could be back in Auckland by tomorrow night. Not early enough to attend that gala function but, to be honest, that added to the appeal of the plan she was formulating.

By the time Olivia Donaldson pulled out of the car park and was headed into rush-hour traffic to get to her central city apartment, she had been online to organise every minute of her day off. She'd also sent Simon a text message.

So sorry but I won't be able to make it tomorrow night after all. Something's come up and I need to head south for the day. It's a personal thing...

CHAPTER TWO

RURAL NEW ZEALAND was a lot wilder and emptier than English countryside.

Olivia Donaldson had had memories of the country's biggest city, Auckland, because she'd lived there until she was about eight years old but she'd never been to a small town like Cutler's Creek.

The main street boasted a church, community hall, petrol station and a pub. A war memorial marked the start of the more intensive commercial area that was, surprisingly, big enough to warrant a decent-sized supermarket amongst cafés and quirky-looking second-hand shops and, on the other side of town before the buildings changed from shops to houses, Olivia spotted the fire station, where an ambulance was parked alongside the fire truck.

She pulled in to stop and stretch her legs after the drive, which had taken a fair bit of concentration—especially that last winding stretch through a gorge. She needed a moment to take a deep breath, too, before she followed the yellow road sign that indicated she would have to turn right off the main road to find the local hospital. Her heels tapped on the paved footpath as she walked a few steps to have a closer look at what seemed to be a deserted emergency response station. Were there people in there, she wondered, or were the firies and ambulance officers here all volunteers who would only come in if needed? She was pretty sure that would be the case. Government funding didn't run to luxuries like paid staff for emergency services in every small town in the back of beyond. It was astonishing, in fact, that Cutler's Creek still had its own hospital.

There was an equally deserted rugby field and clubrooms between the fire station and the first of the small wooden villas that were homes to the local people who weren't farmers. Smoke curled from a chimney or two but no other signs of life. The place was dead. Eerily so, compared to Auckland's bustling inner-city streets. Oh, wait...someone was coming towards Olivia now, on the other side of the road, walking a big, black dog. A middle-aged woman, wearing gumboots and a long, oilskin raincoat, who gave Olivia a hard stare as she went past. Even the dog seemed to be staring at her and it made Olivia feel suddenly even more of a fish out of water. Why had she chosen to wear a tailored pencil skirt and its matching jacket today? Had she really thought that swapping her stilettos for shoes with a lower heel were enough of a nod to country casual?

She turned her back on the woman and lifted her gaze for a moment before she got back into the rental car. She had to admit that the scenery was quite extraordinary with that imposing skyline of snow-peaked mountains looming over the town. On top of being an object of such curiosity for a local, the natural grandeur around Olivia was making her feel rather small and insignificant.

Vulnerable, even? No. She got back into the car and took the next right-hand turn. She had every right to defend herself and she was here to take the bull by the horns, so to speak. Vulnerable people didn't do that kind of thing, did they?

The houses in this new street had big gardens. Some had empty sections beside the houses and there were animals in them. Goats on chains, a pig, a pony wearing a canvas coat to protect it from the weather. The pony Olivia had had as a child had never needed a canvas coat like that. It had lived in a warm stable, as pampered as Olivia had been herself in that exclusive, private boarding school an hour's drive out of London. She hadn't thought of that beloved pony for years and the memory, closely followed by the feeling of loss, was unwelcome—a bit like being poked with a sharp stick.

There was an older man working in a garden as Olivia turned into the grounds of

Cutler's Creek Community Hospital but he stopped for a long moment to lean on his long-handled hoe and watch her drive slowly past.

'*What?*' Olivia muttered aloud. 'Do you never get unannounced visitors here?'

He was wearing gumboots, too. If he turned up on an Auckland street in that footwear, he'd get stared at, as well. Or maybe not. The bigger the city, the harder you had to work to get noticed. Her mother, Janice, had taught her that. She'd been very proud of how much notice Olivia had always garnered. Prizes in her school subjects and in the show-jumping ring at weekends or holidays, top marks at medical school, a career choice in a field as prestigious as plastic surgery and, most recently, for making such a good choice for a life partner in Patrick.

But she hadn't enjoyed the spotlight of being noticed for her own achievements any more than for being her famous mother's daughter. You got stared at when you were under any kind of spotlight and—like this place—the stares always had an element of judgement about them.

How different was this old, sprawling, wooden building that looked like an over-sized villa from the gleaming modern structure that was the private hospital Olivia had been working in only yesterday? There were several parking slots designated for visitors near the front door of the hospital so she took one of them. A quick check of her lipstick in the mirror on the back of the sun flap and Olivia took another deep breath and slammed the car door shut behind her. She might be beginning to have doubts about the wisdom of doing this but she was here now so she might as well get it over with.

The grey-haired, bespectacled woman coming out from behind the desk in the large foyer looked as surprised to see Olivia as the gardener and the dog walker had but at least she wasn't wearing gumboots.

'Can I help you?' she asked.

'I hope so,' Olivia answered. 'I'm here to see Dr Donaldson. Don Donaldson.'

The woman blinked. 'Do you have an appointment?'

Olivia raised her eyebrows, summoning every ounce of confidence she could. 'Do I need one?'

'Ah…' The woman's gaze flicked over Olivia's suit. 'Are you a drug rep?'

A good part of Olivia's confidence was starting to ebb away. Did she look like a drug company representative who was here to peddle her company's drugs or medical products? A salesperson?

'My name,' she said coolly, 'is—'

'Olivia.' The deep voice coming from behind her was astonished. 'It *has* to be.'

Olivia swung around to see who had followed her in through the front door. A tall man, with rather disreputably rumpled hair and looking like he could do with a shave to get rid of that designer stubble, was wearing a white coat over…good grief…*jeans*?

He was looking at her as if she was the last person he'd expected to see standing in the foyer of this hospital. Or the last person he *wanted* to see?

'And you must be Isaac Cameron.'

The curl of one side of his mouth was nothing short of downright cheeky. Impertinent, actually. 'Spot on. How did you guess? I have to admit I had the advantage of having seen your photograph when I stalked you online yesterday.'

It was Olivia's turn to stare. It had been his voice, she realised. That accent with the hint of a Celtic lilt that was even more noticeable in real life. She'd had no idea what the owner of that voice would look like, however, and she was taken aback. More than that. She was more than a bit…gobsmacked, to be honest.

Isaac Cameron had to be *the* most attractive man she had ever seen in her entire life and, as a disconcerting thought that came from nowhere, Olivia wondered why she'd assumed that men like Simon—and Patrick, for that matter—were so good looking because of that groomed, perfect style. This

Isaac Cameron was the complete opposite. He should have had a haircut weeks ago. He had curls of dark hair touching the collar of his white coat and the locks over his forehead had been pushed back, probably with his fingers rather than a comb.

'I don't imagine this hospital is big enough for more than two doctors,' she said calmly. 'And you're not my father.'

The receptionist gasped and then stepped back as if she wanted the protection of being behind her desk again. Olivia could feel an appalled stare scorching her skin. So Dr Cameron wasn't the only person who had judged her and found her to be less than a decent human being? She didn't like being here, Olivia decided. It had been a mistake to come. And, while she might have managed to sound calm, she was feeling anything but.

This was shocking, that's what it was. Or perhaps the shock was that odd tingle that was dancing somewhere deep in Olivia's gut as she made eye contact with a pair of eyes that were the colour of a very rich caramel.

Dear Lord…she was *attracted* to this man?

A whole lot more than she'd ever been attracted to any man in the past?

He clearly wasn't aware of any unwelcome chemical alchemy in the atmosphere. He broke the eye contact instantly to allow his gaze to take in her outfit and the curl of his mouth now suggested that it wasn't at all to his taste but it was exactly what he might have expected her to be wearing. He was making judgements again, wasn't he? About her clothes and her lifestyle. About the relationship she didn't have with her father. About *her*…

'Good to know you remember what he looks like.'

Olivia's breath came out in a startled huff. The hospital receptionist cleared her throat as if she was trying not to laugh. Or convey some kind of warning, perhaps, about who might be overhearing their conversation?

The voice from someone coming into the reception area from an inner corridor was annoyed.

'Ah, there you are, Zac. Where the dickens have you put Geoffrey Watkins's file? I need to see his last ECG.'

The shock wave that shot down Olivia's spine now had nothing whatsoever to do with any physical attraction. She knew this voice almost as well as she knew her own and the sound of it was like a door opening into an entire roomful of memories she didn't want to revisit. Because this man had broken her heart so badly it was never going to be the same. She could never again in her life trust that it was safe to love someone *that* much…

She turned very slowly, steeling herself to face her father.

For his part, Don Donaldson barely gave her a glance before focusing on Isaac as he walked towards them, but then his steps faltered and his gaze returned to Olivia. He went pale. For a split second Olivia felt a beat of fear that the surprise of her visit might actually do physical harm to her father and give him a heart attack or stroke or something. Oddly, the fear made it feel like she had something to lose all over again.

Don opened his mouth and his voice came out as no more than a hoarse whisper. *'Libby?'*

Oh…that hurt with an unexpected ferocity. No one had been allowed to call her that since she'd been about eight years old. *Ever…*

'My name is Olivia,' she said, pronouncing the words as if it was of great importance that they were heard clearly.

'But…but what the hell are you doing *here*?'

Olivia blinked. 'What? This was *your* idea… What *you* wanted…'

Her father was still looking pale. Shocked. Not at all as if his dying wish was being unexpectedly granted.

'Ah…' Isaac held out his hands as if he was about to start directing traffic. 'Let's take this into the staffroom, shall we? I might be able to explain.'

'My office,' Don snapped. 'I don't want any

more of my private business being broadcast, thank you very much.'

The receptionist was being scowled at. She pursed her lips. 'I think you know me better than that, Dr Donaldson.'

His grunt might have been an apology but Olivia was frowning herself as she followed him. This grumpy, older man was a very different person from the father she remembered but perhaps that was a good thing. The past could be left in the past and all she needed to do now was to clear the air of any injustice and get back to where she belonged.

If Isaac Cameron had been wearing a tie, he might have felt the need to loosen it a little as he followed Don Donaldson's daughter into his boss's office. This was his fault but, in his defence, he'd never expected Olivia Donaldson to rock up to this hospital unannounced. On the very next day to him making that phone call? Man, he must have touched a nerve…

And, even though he'd seen her profile

picture on the staff list of the Plastic Surgery Institute in Auckland, he'd never expected that she'd be quite so...so *stunning* in real life. Tall and slim, with that long, honey-blonde hair combed neatly back into a complicated-looking plait. Eyes that were so blue you had to wonder if they were real. He knew she was a well-respected plastic surgeon but she could have had a career as a supermodel if she'd wanted to. It wasn't just her looks, though. There was something about her voice or the way she moved or...perhaps it was her perfume. Whatever... Isaac had never for a moment expected to be attracted to this woman but his body seemed to be defying any orders from his brain right now.

Perhaps it was just an illusion. He was rattled, that's what it was. He hadn't expected her to turn up and now he was responsible for an imminent encounter that was quite likely to be awkward, if not potentially damaging to everybody involved, including himself. Sure enough, Don rounded on Isaac the moment his office door was closed behind the trio.

'You told her, didn't you? After I specifically asked you to keep the information to yourself?'

'Ah…' Technically, Zac had made the call before Don had requested confidentiality but he'd known that he shouldn't be doing it. 'Sorry, Don… I thought it was the right thing to do. That your daughter should know that…'

'That your dying wish was to see me again?' Olivia was shaking her head. 'But that's not actually true, is it?'

Don's eyebrows rose and then lowered even more as he scowled at Isaac. 'You said *that*?'

'I don't remember saying exactly that,' Zac admitted. 'I was a bit riled up on your behalf, though. After seeing all those letters that Olivia had refused to read.'

'I didn't refuse to read them.' Olivia was sounding pretty riled up herself now. 'I never received them. I'm not sure I even believe they exist.'

Zac couldn't help glancing up at the shelf where that filing box was sitting. When he looked down again, he found both Olivia and Don glaring at him and the similarity in their gazes almost made him smile. Clearly father and daughter still had things in common.

'They don't exist any more,' Don muttered. 'I put them through the shredder. But even if they were still in that box, they're just ancient history. Totally irrelevant.'

If he hadn't still been watching Olivia so closely, Zac might have missed the way she swallowed hard just then. Those letters had been important to her, hadn't they? Maybe she was telling the truth and she hadn't known they existed and maybe she'd wanted to see them. There was something about the way she was taking a breath that made him think she was struggling with this. That, despite her very put-together and poised outward appearance, she was actually feeling quite vulnerable. The shrug of her shoulders was definitely defensive.

'I really don't care,' she said. 'But I do believe that seeing me before you died wasn't something on any list of priorities you might have. After all, you've had more than twenty-five years to do something about that. The real reason I came was to tell you it's not fair…'

Yes…there was a tiny wobble in her voice that made Zac wish he'd never made that call. What right had he had to interfere in someone else's life and upset them? And Don was looking alarmingly pale, as if he could collapse at any moment. If he did, it would be entirely Zac's fault. Olivia Donaldson was looking a bit pale herself. Old wounds were being opened here. Deep wounds.

'It's not fair to let people think it was me who rejected you,' Olivia continued. 'When it was totally the other way round. What kind of father just walks out of his kid's life and never looks back?'

He was looking back yesterday, Zac wanted

to say. He was looking back and *crying...* But he kept his mouth shut and said nothing. Because he'd said too much already.

'The lousy kind,' Don said. 'And I don't blame you for hating me. I just don't understand why you've bothered coming all this way to find me.'

'Because someone suggested that I might regret not taking the last chance I'll ever have to see you.' Olivia's chin rose. 'And I decided I wanted to tell you face to face what I thought of you. It's not much, actually. Not as a father. Or as a husband, for that matter. Mum told me how little support she got from you with her career choices. I'm not sure I think much of you as a doctor, either, when you're not even getting proper medical treatment. What kind of example is that to your patients? How can anyone trust you to do what's best for them if you won't even do it for yourself?'

Zac sucked in a breath. Wow... He might have wanted to say something similar to Don himself, but he'd never have delivered it with that much…passion. There were deep feelings there that were showing themselves in anger but he could feel something very different beneath what was showing. He could almost see a small girl who was bewildered and hurt because her father had abandoned her.

What on earth had made Don do something so appalling? There was a part of him who wanted to step in and simply give Olivia a hug. But he could imagine how unwelcome that would be. He shouldn't even be in this room. This was none of his business.

Don must have been reading his mind.

'This is none of your business,' he growled. Except that he was talking to Olivia, not Zac. 'I didn't ask you to come here. You shouldn't have come. You don't belong here, any more than your mother did. Why don't you just get out while the going's good?'

Oh, no… Zac found he was holding his breath. Could things get any worse?

Apparently, they could.

'Oh, don't worry.' Olivia was already turning on her heel. 'That's precisely what I'm going to do.'

Zac had to steel himself to meet Don's gaze as the door slammed behind his daughter. He knew he was going to be facing a man who had every right to be very angry with him.

Except he didn't look angry. He looked… as sad as anyone Zac had ever seen.

'You can go, too,' he said quietly. 'Just leave me alone, okay?'

Her hands were shaking so much that it took two attempts to get the rental car started. And then Olivia found that her vision was blurred by tears so she had to pull over, not far from where she'd stopped not so long ago, near the fire station. She swiped at her face and hauled in one deep breath after another as she tried to calm down. Why on earth was she so upset? Had she expected anything else from the man who'd walked out of her life when she was far too young to understand what might have driven him to do that? Had she had some deeply hidden hope that she might discover that her father did still love her, like that stranger had suggested in his phone message?

Of course he didn't. He hadn't expressed any desire to even see her before he died. That was simply a flight of fancy by someone who'd had no business interfering. Stirring up things that would have best been left alone. And, yes, it hurt but it was a pain Olivia had had plenty of practice dealing with. She'd had it nailed by the time she was in her early teens so nothing had really changed. She'd made a mistake by coming here, that was all, and the best that she could do now to repair the damage was to get away from this place as quickly as possible and try to just forget about it. At least she'd left the township behind now. There was farmland on either side of the road and she was heading towards the narrow, winding road that led through the gorge.

Not that it was going to be easy to push those stupidly intense minutes out of her head, she realised a few minutes later. It wasn't just that horrible conversation with her father, because she was already pushing that into the part of her brain where everything else to do with Donald Donaldson had been buried. No… There was another man whose image it might be even harder to erase. The troublemaker. Some kind of irresponsible bad boy who'd fallen into a forgotten corner of her life and had decided to wreak havoc.

It was quite possible she was going to be thinking about Isaac Cameron for a rather long time. Wondering why she'd never felt anything quite like that kind of tingle deep in her belly before and whether she would ever feel it again. That pull of sheer…desire that even thinking about the man could generate.

Good grief… Olivia shook her head. It wasn't just an electrical jolt she could feel in her body, she could hear a loud humming in her ears that was getting rapidly louder. So loud, she found herself looking up. And then she was stamping on the brake pedal and bringing her car to a complete halt as a single-engine light plane came from no-where, only a short distance ahead of her, crossing the road barely above the level of her car's roof. Its engine was roaring as it gained some height and then it coughed and spluttered and the plane dipped again. What was the pilot trying to do—make an emergency landing in a farmer's field? If so, it needed to get a lot higher than it was, to clear the dense macrocarpa pine trees in the wind-break and how was it going to do that if its engine was dying?

Olivia watched in horror as the plane's wheels dragged through a treetop and then its wings tipped one way and then the other as it got rapidly closer to the ground, sheep scattering to get away from the overhead in-trusion. It bounced as a wheel touched the ground but then the small aircraft rolled, nosedived and finally came to a shockingly abrupt halt upside down. Olivia sat there, frozen, for a moment and then jumped out of her car, her phone in her hand. She punched in the three-digit code for the emergency services.

'Where is your emergency?'

'I'm on State Highway One. About ten minutes out of Cutler's Creek, heading towards Dunedin.'

'What's happened?'

'It's a plane. It's crashed into a paddock. Small plane, a Cessna, maybe.'

'Do you have any idea of how many people are involved?'

'No… I couldn't see inside when it went over me.'

'What can you see now?'

'Um…' There was a puff of smoke coming from where the plane had crashed but Olivia was too far away to see whether there was any movement inside or around the plane. 'I can't see anything.' She needed to get closer but there was a barbed-wire fence and a ditch she would need to cross.

'Stay on the line,' she was told. 'Help's on its way.'

Olivia was looking up and down the road.

How long was it going to take for that help to arrive? Surely someone would come past and be able to assist her with a first response? From the direction she'd come from, she could hear the faint wail of a civil defence siren. Were the local volunteer fire brigade and ambulance officers being summoned to the station?

Even if they were, it was going to take them at least several minutes to get here. Possibly crucial minutes if there were lives that were hanging in the balance. Someone with an arterial bleed, perhaps. Or now trapped upside down in a position that was occluding their airway. Olivia was a doctor—she couldn't stand here and do nothing, even though the prospect of being first on this scene was actually rather terrifying. She'd worked in emergency departments with all the equipment and staff available to back up or take over an attempt to save a life but here…here she was entirely on her own and in a huge space with those towering mountains in the background that were still making her feel insignificant and she had nothing and no-body to help and…

It was possibly the first time in her life that Olivia Donaldson had to rely entirely on herself and her own judgement and to act so fast it had to be based on instinct as well as any skills she had learned over the years. Those skills didn't include getting over a fence with barbed wire on the top but Olivia pulled apart two strands lower down on the fence, put her head through and then one leg and somehow the rest of her body followed easily enough, although she could feel the side seam of her narrow skirt catch and rip a little. She set off across the uneven grassed land at a run and all she was thinking about as she got closer to the plane was how she was going to try and get the doors open and how badly hurt the occupants might be and how on earth she was going to get them out and look after them with nothing more than her bare hands.

Slowing down as she got close to the plane wasn't just to catch her breath. Long ago, at medical school, Olivia had attended an interesting workshop that paramedics had given about being first on the scene at any emergency. Snippets were drifting back into her head and she knew that the first thing she had to do was to assess the scene for any dangers to herself and any other rescuers that would be arriving. Things like broken glass or leaking fuel that could present a fire hazard or power lines that were down. A glance back towards the road confirmed that nearby power lines seemed to still be intact.

It also showed Olivia that a vehicle with a flashing light on its roof had come through the gate of this huge paddock further down the road. It wasn't a fire truck or an ambulance. It looked like an SUV and the light was one of those magnetic temporary ones. Someone was driving rapidly towards her. It should have been far too far away to recognise the driver but Olivia had no doubt at all about who it was.

Isaac Cameron.

It didn't matter that it was the person who

had just stirred up a part of her past that should have been left well alone. She had never been so pleased at the prospect of seeing anyone in her whole life.

She wasn't facing this alone, after all.

CHAPTER THREE

ISAAC CAMERON HAD never expected to see this woman again.

She wouldn't have been his first choice to work with in an emergency situation, either, but—fair play—when he'd arrived, he'd seen how hard she'd been running across this paddock with the obvious intention of helping whoever was in this plane. As he pulled his vehicle to a halt and leapt out to get his medical pack from the back, part of his brain registered that she must have ripped that tight skirt of her power suit getting past the barbed wire on the fence and she probably wouldn't appreciate the fact that her careful hairstyle was coming a little unravelled and that she was now well splattered with animal manure but, in this moment, her appearance was totally irrelevant to either of them.

'Did you see it come down?' Zac dropped his pack near a wingtip and bent to get beneath the diagonal strut that connected the wing to the fuselage of the small aircraft.

'Yes. It went right in front of my car.'

'So it was trying to land?' Zac could see the slumped figure of a man in the cockpit.

'I think so. It sounded like there was something wrong with the engine. The wheels got caught in the trees. It flipped over right at the last second and there was a bang when it stopped so suddenly.'

Zac wasn't surprised. The propeller had dug itself deep into the soil. The Plexiglas of the windshield was broken, too, and there were splatters of blood on it. He leaned to look in further.

'I can't see any passengers. I think it's just the pilot.' He rapped on the side window. 'Hello…can you hear me? I'm a doctor. We're here to help you.'

'Is…is he still alive?'

She sounded as if she really cared.

'He's not responding.' He tried the door.

It opened an inch or two but then stuck. He braced his back against the strut and wrenched harder. With a third attempt and the screech of metal against metal he shifted the door enough to reach the victim. He eased him back, upright enough to ensure that his airway was open, keeping hold of his head to protect his neck. A trickle of blood rolled down the man's forehead from an injury hidden in his hair. That could be where the blood on the windscreen had come from, which meant there was a potential head injury to be concerned about. The man groaned loudly as he was moved.

'What's hurting, mate?' The man wasn't local, which was a relief. In a small place like Cutler's Creek, an accident scene often meant they were treating someone they knew well and Isaac knew exactly how devastating that could be—like that time their local police officer had arrived at a car accident involving his own son.

On a personal level for Zac, any emergency scene carried the threat of a flashback, along with a memory of Mia. It was no wonder he'd been able to start shutting down the ability to care too much after that—a skill that might have ended up being too well honed but was still useful in some situations, like when he'd had to work on Bruce's son, but it was always easier when the patient was a stranger. And the really disturbing flashbacks had stopped long ago.

'My back...' the man groaned. 'And my leg...'

'Are you having any trouble breathing?'

'Hurts...'

Zac could hear that his breathing was rapid and shallow but it was too cramped to try and assess anything in here.

'What's your name?'

'Dave... Wilson.' He groaned again and tried to roll his head away from Zac's grip. He tightened his hold to limit the movement.

'Do you know where you are?'

'I... It's... Oh, God...what's happened?'

'You've been in an accident. Try not to move, Dave,' Zac told him. 'We're going to get you out of here, okay?' He turned his head to meet a wide-eyed gaze from Olivia. She looked scared, he thought, and he could understand why. Used to the clean environment of first-world hospitals and a team around her, she was a long way out of her comfort zone right now. But her determination was obvious in the way she pulled back a tress of her hair that the wind had caught and shoved it behind one ear as she raised her chin. She wasn't about to let any nerves get in the way of what needed to be done.

'There's a cervical collar clipped to the side of my pack, there. Could you pass it to me, please?'

'Sure.'

He had the plastic and foam collar in his hands seconds later and he carefully slipped it into place and fastened the Velcro straps.

'*Ow...*'

'Sorry, mate. I know it's not comfortable but we need to protect your neck. We'll get you something for the pain as soon as we get you out.'

We...

As if they were a team? Zac knew the local first response would be on their way already. He could hear voice traffic on the radio that was clipped to the dashboard of his vehicle but he couldn't hear what was being said. He needed to update the emergency services as soon as he could to make sure a rescue helicopter had been dispatched but, yes...for the moment, he and Don Donaldson's daughter felt like a team.

Still keeping a protective hand on the man's forehead, he reached for the fastening of the safety harness with his other hand.

'Dammit...'

'What is it?'

'I can't reach the catch.'

'Maybe I can.' Olivia spoke before he could make the same suggestion.

She had to squeeze past him into the narrow space he'd created. She was pressed right against his body by the time she was reaching in, trying to follow the safety harness to its catch.

'Be careful. There's sharp stuff in here.'

'He's bleeding. A lot.'

'Where from?'

'I can't see… Lower leg, maybe.'

'We need to get him out. Stat.'

'I can feel the catch but…it's not working.'

Zac saw the way her forehead furrowed with the effort she was making. And the way she caught her bottom lip between her teeth. She was pressing even harder against him, making it impossible for him to move that arm.

'My back pocket.'

'What?'

'I've got a multi-tool in the back pocket of my jeans. Get it out and we'll cut the harness.'

He felt her fingers slide into his pocket. He shouldn't have been thinking of anything but looking after his patient's cervical spine, watching any movements of his chest to try and assess just how much difficulty the pilot was having breathing, and planning ahead for the urgent assessment and treatment that would be needed the moment they could free their patient from the wreckage, but…

…but it felt as if there was no layer of denim between those fingers and the bare skin of his buttock and, just for a nanosecond, Zac was aware of…heat. Skin-scorching, spine-tingling *heat*… And it was the first time he'd felt even a hint of something like that since… Oh… *God*… It wasn't just an emergency scene that could bring back a memory of Mia, was it? He might not want to be someone who felt nothing at all but the pendulum swinging too far the other way—to huge emotions that could prove impossible to control—was just as undesirable.

'Take that cap off the side.' His command came out as a snap. 'See that V-shaped notch?'

'Yes.'

'Put the edge of the safety belt into that notch and just pull. Mind your fingers, it's sharp.'

Zac was holding onto the pilot with both hands to steady both his neck and his body as Olivia sliced through the heavy straps. Despite how nervous she'd looked when he'd arrived at this scene, she hadn't hesitated in following his instructions, he noticed, and she'd checked to see that their patient was supported before she cut the second strap. Then, in what seemed like an automatic gesture, she recapped the sharp implement and slipped it into the pocket of her jacket.

She was thorough, he thought. And pretty courageous, given the way she had virtually climbed into this wreck to help. Moments later, as Olivia took the weight of Dave's legs as Zac lifted his upper body, keeping him as straight as possible as they eased him to the ground beside the plane, he had to add an impression of surprising strength that this woman had.

There were so many things that needed to be done. The cries of pain from Dave let Zac know that his airway was still clear but he needed to be on oxygen to compensate for any breathing difficulty and he needed pain relief as soon as possible, which meant getting an IV line in. He needed to have any severe bleeding controlled and, given how agitated he was, it might well be necessary to sedate and intubate him so that they could transport him safely.

Zac could hear the siren of the first local response getting closer but while the volunteers here were well trained for fire-fighting and a basic level of first aid, he had to hope that Olivia Donaldson's clinical skills were on the same level as her courage and strength.

She'd never seen anyone work like this.

Isaac Cameron only had the contents of his pack to work with until the local ambulance arrived but you would have thought he was in a resuscitation area of a well-equipped emergency department given how smoothly he was using his resources.

Including her, along with the two ambulance officers that arrived within minutes of them getting Dave out of the wreckage of his plane. It was Olivia who was doing the most to assist, however, as the most qualified extra medic on the scene. She was the one who put an IV line into their patient's arm while Zac was busy assessing both Dave's head and chest injuries. She drew up the drugs needed for pain relief as the paramedics controlled the bleeding from an open fracture of his lower leg.

One of them looked up. 'D'you guys smell that?'

Zac unhooked his stethoscope from his ears and inhaled sharply. 'You're right, Ben. We've got a fuel leak happening somewhere.'

'At least the firies are on their way. I can hear their siren.'

'We still need to move him.' The other young man jumped to his feet. 'I'll get the scoop.'

'Move back,' Zac ordered Olivia. 'At least to the other side of the ambulance. This isn't safe.'

'It's never been safe.' She shook her head. 'And I'm not going anywhere.' She leaned towards Dave's head. 'Are you allergic to any medicine you know of, Dave?'

'Don't think so… Oh, *God*…it still hurts…'

'I know. I'm about to give you something for that. It might make you feel a bit woozy.' Olivia flicked the syringe and then pressed the plunger to expel any air, removing the needle and attaching the syringe to the Luer plug but glancing up before she actually injected the drug. She knew Zac was watching her and it was polite to get his permission before going any further. As bizarre as this situation was, it was *his* territory and he was in charge here.

He held her gaze for the split second it took for him to nod and she could see something more than permission to administer the drugs in that look. Respect, perhaps? Whatever it was, it felt good enough for any residual nerves at having to work in such unusual circumstances to dissipate almost entirely.

The paramedics had a bright orange, plastic stretcher that was separated into two pieces.

'We're going to roll him to each side and

slip the stretcher together underneath to clip together,' Zac told her. 'We need to be careful to keep spinal alignment, okay? I've got his head. You take his upper arm and the guys will do the rest. Ready? On the count of three. One…two…*three*…'

Carefully, but swiftly, they log-rolled the pilot to one side enough to get half the stretcher in place and then they repeated the procedure on the other side. Olivia had to scramble to her feet, then, as the three men, working as a well-oiled team, lifted the stretcher and shifted it rapidly to a safer area of the paddock. Olivia gathered up as much of the gear as she could and ran after them. She could see the fire engine coming into the paddock but then she heard the *whoosh* of fuel igniting behind them, felt the instant blast of heat from the flames and she missed her footing and fell.

No…she hadn't tripped, she realised a split second later. She'd been grabbed and pushed and she still had a pair of strong, male arms around her body. A body virtually on top of hers, in fact, but that wasn't as startling as the eyes that were so close to her own. Caramel-coloured eyes that had such an intense expression that Olivia's heart skipped a beat. Was it *fear* she was seeing?

Whatever it was, it was gone in another heartbeat. Zac scrambled to his feet and offered her a hand to get up.

'Sorry about that. I wasn't sure how close we were to that explosion, that's all.'

So he'd thrown himself on top of her to protect her?

Wow... Olivia felt the need to suck in a deep breath.

'You're not hurt, are you?' The query was concerned but she could see that Isaac's head was turning towards where their patient had been placed.

'No. I just got a bit of a fright, that's all.' A glance at the flames engulfing the wreckage of the plane made Olivia realise that she was still rather nervous but she remembered how little Isaac had thought of her when he'd left that voicemail on her phone and she didn't want him to think she was pathetic, as well.

Except he didn't seem to. There was understanding in his gaze now. And more of what she'd seen before that had given her so much confidence. That look that made her think he might actually be impressed.

'It's okay. Our firies will get that sorted. We're safe here.'

Sure enough, the fire engine had reached the plane wreckage now and there were people running and shouting as they readied their gear to deal with the fire. The gate to the paddock had been left open behind them, Olivia noticed, and a mob of panicked sheep was now streaming out onto the main road. Perhaps their patient was aware of the chaos around him because he had suddenly become more agitated as Zac and Olivia reached him.

'Dave? Can you hear me?' Ben was speaking loudly. 'Don't move… *Dave?*'

'He's not responding.' Zac seemed oblivious to anything else that was going on around them as he turned swiftly back to lean over the stretcher and check Dave's level of consciousness. Olivia could see that he wasn't opening his eyes and his speech had become no more than incoherent groaning.

Zac had asked one of the paramedics to radio for an update. 'How far away is the chopper?'

'Ten to fifteen minutes,' Ben told him.

'I'm going to do a rapid sequence intubation,' Zac said. 'His LOC is dropping and he's not going to be safe to transport if he's this agitated.'

The young paramedic reached for a plastic pouch in the pack beside her. He glanced at Zac, who nodded in Olivia's direction.

'You happy to assist me with an RSI?' he asked.

'Of course.' Olivia held her hands out to take the pouch that she could see contained the drugs and instruments that would be needed for the procedure. Having enjoyed her training in anaesthetics so much as a junior doctor, she was very familiar with every aspect of the use of strong drugs to sedate a patient and then the sometimes tricky task of easing a tube into the trachea to protect an airway and take over someone's breathing. She had only ever done it in the anteroom of a sterile operating theatre, mind you, with any number of staff and all the equipment that might be needed if something went wrong. The thought of doing it in the middle of a paddock, with smouldering plane wreckage in the background and people yelling from the road where they were trying to deal with the mob of sheep now causing a traffic hazard was…well, it was actually rather exciting.

Thrilling, even, Olivia decided minutes later as she injected the drug that was going to paralyse Dave and watched Zac as he knelt behind the pilot's head and focused on the procedure, ready to assist with whatever else he needed her to do, like putting pressure on the cricoid cartilage at the front of the neck to aid tube placement. He had to use both hands, one manipulating the laryngoscope and the other inserting the endotracheal tube, and it felt like only seconds later that he was attaching the bag mask and holding that with one hand to provide ventilation as he used his stethoscope with his other hand to listen to breath sounds and check that the tube placement was correct. The whole procedure had been so swift and smooth that Olivia could feel her jaw dropping.

Wow… How clever were this man's hands? And how confident was he?

The rescue helicopter was coming in to land by the time they had secured the tube and made sure that all the measurements they were monitoring were acceptable. A smaller helicopter was not far behind it.

'News crew,' someone said. 'National TV.'

The air rescue aircraft landed well away from where they were working but Olivia could feel the chop of the rotors beating in her own body. They didn't shut down the engine because the crew knew their patient had already been stabilised and they would be able to take off again within minutes.

They also seemed to know Zac well and he got waves and thumbs-up signals before the doors were shut and the aircraft took off again. The news crew was hovering nearby, clearly filming the accident scene and the final moments of the pilot's rescue, before swinging away.

The beat of rotors increased as the air rescue chopper lifted off and Zac turned as his hand dropped from the wave he'd been returning. His gaze caught Olivia's as they both turned to begin walking back to where his vehicle was parked near the ambulance, and maybe he was feeling the same kind of adrenaline rush that she was at being part of this extraordinary incident, because he smiled at her. A kind of lop-sided, almost grin that lit up his face and somehow coalesced with the vibration of the sound from the helicopter into something that Olivia could feel right down to her bones and then radiating out in an intensified version of the tingle she'd been aware of when she'd first set eyes on this man. It wasn't just this crazy situation or the rush of having worked to try and save someone's life that was thrilling, was it?

There was something about Isaac Cameron that was threatening to become the most memorable aspect of this brief, unexpected interruption to Olivia's life, and that was disturbing enough to make her break the eye contact without returning that smile. She glanced at her watch as if knowing the time of day was of the utmost importance. Which, of course, it was.

'Oh...*no...*'

'Problem?' Zac wasn't smiling any more.

'I haven't got a hope of getting back to Dunedin in time to catch my flight.'

A hint of that smile made one side of his mouth twitch and Olivia glared at him. He was finding this amusing? But Zac was oblivious to her glare because he wasn't looking at her face. How rude was that, to be eyeing her body up and down like some cheeky teenaged boy?

'Don't suppose you brought a change of clothes with you?'

'What?' Olivia hadn't given a thought to what state she was in but Zac's comment gave her a vague recollection of ripping her skirt on that barbed-wire fence. She looked down and then closed her eyes for a heartbeat as she groaned aloud. Her clothes weren't just ripped—they were filthy, with streaks of dirt and blood and...good grief...sheep manure? Those shoes would never be the same.

The paramedics were loading the last of their gear back into the ambulance.

'We put your pack in the back of your car, Zac,' Ben called.

'Thanks, mate.'

'See you soon, yeah? Training session tomorrow night?'

'Sure thing—as long as the weather doesn't get too gnarly.'

'True. If that storm gets here early we might be busy rescuing people, not training. Either way, we'll be seeing you soon.'

The firies were also packing up their gear,

preparing to leave, as Olivia and Zac neared his SUV. A police car coming into the paddock slowed and then stopped as it got close. The driver's window rolled down.

'Hey, Zac... Bit of excitement for you, I hear?'

'Yep. If you need a statement, though, Dr Donaldson here is your woman, Bruce. She witnessed the crash.'

'Dr Donaldson?' The older man blinked but then collected himself. 'Yes, a statement would be great. I'm going to be on site until the Civil Aviation investigators arrive. They'll want to talk to her as well, I expect.' He shifted his gaze to Olivia. 'You staying for a while?'

'No. I'm on my way back to Auckland. That's my car out there...' Olivia pointed to the road. She could only see the roof of her car because it was surrounded by sheep.

'It would be helpful if you could stay long enough to give a statement.'

'And you might want to have a shower and get your clothes washed before you go anywhere,' Zac added. 'Come back to the hospital with me and we'll get you sorted.'

'No *way.*' Olivia was not going near Cutler's Creek Community Hospital again. Ever. She could still hear that dismissive tone of her father's voice telling her that she shouldn't have come in the first place. That she should get out while the going was good. She hadn't forgotten the stares of strangers, either. Curious but vaguely judgemental. Like the look on this police officer's face right now as he took a notebook from his shirt pocket.

'Be a good idea to stay in town for a few hours,' he advised. 'Perhaps you can give me your phone number so I can get in touch when the investigators get here. Hopefully it won't be too long.' He wrote down the number that Olivia recited and then nodded at Zac before driving closer to the plane wreckage.

'Keep me posted,' was all he said.

Zac raised an eyebrow at Olivia. 'How 'bout my place, instead? Not so far from here. Far enough away from town. I've got to head back to work but you'd be welcome to use my shower. And I've got a washing machine.' The corner of his mouth quirked again, making her think that this man was far too easily amused. 'I've even got Wi-Fi. You might be able to change your ticket and get a later plane tonight. And you won't be running from the law without providing your statement. Not that I expect you'd ever do anything remotely illegal...'

There was something confusing about this man, Olivia realised. At times he seemed completely laid-back and confident. At other times, he was judgemental and aloof. Arrogant, even, like he had been when he'd left that voicemail on her phone? But there'd been that moment after the plane wreckage had exploded and she could have sworn she'd seen what had looked like fear in his eyes. Or horror, even. What had that been about?

She had to admit she was curious but she was also busy weighing up her options. She couldn't simply drive off into the sunset.

Quite apart from being obliged to speak to the people who would be investigating this crash, there was no way she could go anywhere looking like this. There might be a shop in town that would sell clothing but she'd already had enough of people staring at her. Besides, she hadn't realised until now how cold the wind was and the thought of a hot shower in the not-too-distant future was more than appealing. Even if there was a motel available in this small town, it would take time to find it. Isaac Cameron was offering her by far the best possible solution, she realised. And maybe she could justify her willingness to accept as a case of better the devil you knew?

'Fine,' she said ungraciously. 'I could use your place. As long as you won't be there.' Both Zac's eyebrows were raised now and Olivia suddenly felt ashamed of herself. 'Thanks,' she muttered. 'I appreciate the offer.'

'Least I can do,' Zac said calmly. 'I appreciated your help here. Reckon we might have saved that guy's life, don't you?'

Olivia caught her bottom lip between her teeth. She didn't want Zac to know how proud it made her feel that he'd found her assistance helpful. Or that potentially saving a life was the most satisfying thing she had done medically in rather a long time. She made a vague sound of agreement, however, as she turned her head to look again at the hundreds of sheep milling around her rental car.

'How am I going to get to my car?'

He was grinning. 'You're a real city girl, aren't you?'

Actually, no, Olivia wanted to tell him. I got sent away to boarding school when I was only five and it was out in the country. There were plenty of sheep around there. And then my mother found me another boarding school in the countryside in England and I even had my own pony, but you know what? I'd rather have been a city girl. Living with my own family…

But it wasn't any of his business and she wasn't about to tell him something that he might relate to her father—the man who had probably been happy to agree with her mother and send her away in the first place—so Olivia said nothing.

Zac's grin faded and then he shrugged. 'The sheep won't bother you, I promise. Someone will round them up and get them back in here as soon as we've gone. Jump in…' He held the passenger door of his SUV open. 'I'll get you back to your car and then you can just follow me.'

Thank goodness he'd done a bit of housework over the last few days. The kitchen bench wasn't piled with its usual collection of used pots and plates and there were clean towels available. Zac led the way into a hallway, opened a cupboard and handed two of the towels to Olivia.

'Bathroom's down the end of the hall. There's plenty of stuff like shampoo. Probably not what you're used to but it'll do the job. If you need something to wear while you wash your stuff, try the bottom drawer of the tallboy in my bedroom. There's a bunch of old track pants and jeans and sweatshirts that I only use for training days. They'll be a bit big but they're all clean and they should keep you warm.' He didn't want to think about what Olivia might or might not be wearing under any borrowed clothes. He didn't want to think about her standing in his shower, either. Totally naked…

The sooner he got back to the hospital, the better. 'I'll throw a couple of new logs in the pot belly stove in the kitchen. I don't have a dryer but if you put your clothes on the rack above the stove, they'll dry in no time.'

'Thanks.' Olivia was following him as he went to poke the fire back into life. 'Do you have a code for your Wi-Fi?'

'Yep. It's pinned to that corkboard there.'

'Do you want to me to lock up when I leave?'

'I never bother. Pretty safe place, Cutler's Creek.' Zac closed the door of the stove after putting more fuel into it. Maybe it was the lick of new flames he could see that were making him feel so on edge again. They were reminders of both unexpected heat and potentially dangerous explosions.

Yeah…he was a lot more rattled than he wanted to think about. 'Right, then… I'd better go. I'll let Bruce know where he can find you when they're ready for that statement.'

'I'd better get on with cleaning myself up.' Unexpectedly, she smiled at him. 'Thanks again, Zac.'

Oh, wow…it was the first time he'd seen any hint of a smile on her face and it was some smile. Generous and warm and it made her lips curve into the most enchanting shape ever. He'd already realised that Olivia Donaldson was quite possibly the most beautiful woman he'd ever met in real life but that smile just took the package to a whole new level and that was even more disturbing than whatever heat and fear had been flickering along with those flames.

His mouth went dry as he turned away, so

he didn't say anything by way of a farewell, just raised his hand as he left. It was a good thing that she wouldn't be here by the time he got home again in a few hours' time. It was going to take some time and effort to get past the ripples of disturbance this woman had been a part of today. Zac had the feeling he could well be haunted by echoes that were unlikely to fade any time soon.

If ever...

CHAPTER FOUR

To SEE THAT small red rental car still parked outside his barn when he drove home was a surprise, to say the least.

Zac was trying to decide whether his heart rate had picked up because the surprise was a pleasant one, rather than a potential problem, when he walked inside his house to find Olivia in his kitchen, wearing a pair of his ancient track pants and a sweatshirt with the sleeves rolled up. This was even more disconcerting, especially when the scent of the shampoo and soap she had used was so familiar it made it seem like she belonged here. She had not only washed her hair, which was hanging in loose waves down her back, she had also washed off any makeup she'd been wearing. She should have looked a lot less attractive but, in fact, the opposite was true.

Olivia Donaldson not only still looked impossibly gorgeous but now seemed far more approachable—with a girl-next-door vibe instead of a supermodel pretending to be a private surgeon.

So, okay…maybe the surprise *was* pleasant. Especially given that Zac had recovered from the rattled sensation he'd had after that accident scene and that Olivia's antagonism seemed to have worn off for the time being.

'Sorry,' she said to him by way of a greeting. 'I meant to be gone long ago but I was waiting for the wash cycle to finish and then those people from the crash investigation turned up and I forgot to take things out to put on the rack…' Her nose crinkled to give her an apologetic expression. '…and I'm still here…'

'So I see.' Zac had been caught by that nose crinkling thing, which had offered a glimpse of a very different side to the sophisticated woman who had turned up in his hospital earlier this afternoon. 'No problem. Did you manage to change your flight?'

'Yes, but I couldn't get another one till early afternoon tomorrow. I've been online trying to find a motel nearby but the only place within a hundred miles or so seems to be the pub, is that right?'

'Yeah...' Should he warn her that word had got out that Don Donaldson's daughter had turned up to visit him only to storm off again, slamming the door behind her like a spoilt child, and that the community of Cutler's Creek wasn't exactly impressed? That he was thinking it wasn't such a good idea for her to stay at the pub must have shown in his face because Olivia shook her head and her breath came out in a tiny snort.

'I was wondering about that. They're not going to welcome the prodigal daughter, right? Guess I'll hit the road and find a motel in Dunedin, then.'

'It's getting dark. I wouldn't advise driving through that gorge when you're not familiar with the road. Especially with this wind picking up.'

'Oh...'

She was looking slightly anxious now and, along with that uncontrolled hair and the way that no makeup made her look years younger, it gave the impression of a vulnerability that tugged at something deep within Zac. And then something else blindsided him completely. She might look like this first thing in the morning, he thought, when she was waking up all rumpled from sleep in a strange bed after the first night of passionate sex with a new lover. Out of her comfort zone and wondering about the best way to handle things? *Oh...* Zac actually felt slightly weak at the knees. Imagine being that man. That lucky, *lucky* man...

Was it his imagination or did Olivia's pupils suddenly dilate to make her eyes look an even darker shade of blue? The way the tip of her tongue came out to moisten her lips was certainly not a figment of his imagination and it had an instant effect on his body that had nothing to do with his knees. So did that husky note in her voice. Was it possible that Olivia was just as aware of the sudden sexual tension in the atmosphere as he was?

'What *would* you advise, then?'

For a crazy few seconds, ludicrous things that Zac would very much have liked to suggest bounced around inside his skull. Not in words so much as an urge to simply pull this woman into his arms and cover her lips with his own to see if it was possible that she tasted as good as she looked. He wanted to kiss her senseless. To pick her up and carry her off to his bedroom, like some sort of caveman. Of course, he wasn't going to do any of those things. That would be a huge mistake.

It wasn't that he'd lived like a monk since he'd lost Mia. Far from it. But this felt different. For one thing, Olivia Donaldson was the daughter of his boss—a man he respected a great deal. For another, sex for Zac for years now had been a connection that was nothing more than something physical. And transient. This woman was making him feel

things that were too intense to be comfortable and that made her…dangerous?

No. Zac had this under control. He even
managed to keep his tone perfectly casual
as he deliberately turned away to peer out
of the kitchen window.

'I'm sure we can think of something by the
time your clothes are dry. If the worst comes
to the worst, there's a spare bed here.'

Dear Lord…the way he had *looked* at her
even though it had only been for a matter of
a second. Two, tops. But nobody had ever
looked at her like that. As if nothing else in
the world existed. As if he wanted to drag
her off by her hair and have his wicked way
with her.

Oh, *my*…

Olivia could feel colour flooding into her
cheeks. Thank goodness she was looking at
Zac's back now as he looked out of the window. Her heart rate had picked up so much
it felt like he would have been able to see it
making her chest jump despite the gener-

ous covering of the oversized sweatshirt and surely nobody could have missed that blush.

She couldn't possibly stay in the same house as this man because she knew what could very well happen. And that couldn't be allowed to happen because random sexual encounters with complete strangers had never, ever been acceptable to Olivia and she wasn't about to start breaking her own moral code now. She hadn't even slept with Patrick until he'd made it very clear that he was serious about a significant relationship with her.

But…there was a tiny voice in the back of her head telling her that Patrick had never looked at her like that. That no man had. That maybe she would never find anyone else who would. And she couldn't deny that there was a strong sense of curiosity, as well. If a man could do that to you, just with his eyes, what could he be capable of doing with his hands? Or his tongue…or…or…

'You might be right about the drive…' Olivia had to clear her throat. How embar-

rassing was that—to sound so husky? 'But…
I can't stay here.'

Of course she could, that little voice insisted. It would only be one night of her life
and nobody else ever needed to know about
it. Besides…maybe nothing would happen.
Maybe she had imagined that look.

'Up to you.' Zac turned away from the
window. 'You've got a bit of time to think
about it while your clothes are drying, anyway. I'll be outside for a bit. I need to go and
see Chloe.'

'Chloe?' Olivia blinked. Was there another
woman around here somewhere? A neighbour perhaps…or a girlfriend? And how
ridiculous was it that the thought was so dis-
appointing?

'You haven't noticed the biggest horse in
the world in the back garden?' Zac opened
the fridge and took out a handful of carrots.
As he closed the door, there was a gentle
clinking sound from wine bottles stored in
a rack on top of the fridge. 'Feel free to open

one of those, if you like,' he added. 'You'll find the corkscrew in the drawer by the sink.'

A combination of the emotional upheaval of that encounter with her father and then the adrenaline rush of helping with the emergency response at the accident scene on top of the fatigue of a very early start for all that travelling made the prospect of a glass of wine irresistible. Not that Olivia was about to admit it, even to herself, but there was also the bonus that if she had a glass of wine or two, the decision of whether or not she needed to stay off the road for the night would be made for her.

Putting the corkscrew back into the drawer after dealing with a cork, Olivia glanced out the window to see Zac with the carrots in one hand and a biscuit of hay under his other arm, walking towards a wooden gate beneath an archway of hedge that made a perfect frame for the horse that was standing there. With the background of snow-peaked mountains, the image looked like a postcard and there was something about the beauty of it that actually brought a lump to her throat. Gusts of wind were stealing wisps of the hay and she could hear the welcoming sounds the horse was making as it saw food and company arriving. That sound was enough to make Olivia have to blink away a sudden prickle behind her eyes.

It was another memory that had been long locked away. That soft nicker of equine pleasure and the joy that was contagious. She could almost feel the warmth of her beloved pony Koko and smell the distinctive scent that had always been there as she'd wrapped her arms around his neck and buried her face against his skin. It was a memory that tugged at her heartstrings enough to be painful.

Rather like the memories she'd already fielded earlier today that were connected to the father she'd remembered. A man who didn't seem to exist any more. Maybe her memories weren't actually real. Had she, in fact, created memories of the kind of man any child would have wanted her father to have been?

Olivia took a huge gulp of the glass of wine she had just poured as she continued staring out the window. Zac had opened the gate and the horse was rubbing its huge head on his arm. It *was* a huge horse. Zac had to be at least a few inches over six feet tall but his head didn't reach Chloe's shoulder. Daylight was fading fast but that only made the horse's fluffy white feet and the blaze on her nose more obvious.

'Is Chloe a Clydesdale?' she asked when Zac came back into the kitchen.

'Not purebred, I was told, but close enough.'

'Do you ride her?'

Zac laughed. 'Are you kidding? I'd need a ladder to get on board. And it would be a long way to fall off. Besides…she might be pregnant. Apparently.'

'Apparently?'

'She came with the house. The guy who owns this place is overseas and he wanted someone to look after things, including the hens and his horse, but I've been here for nearly a year and there's no sign of any baby so I think he's going to be disappointed.' Zac was looking at her empty glass. 'Want a refill?'

'Um...' This was decision time. A second glass would mean she wasn't going to be driving anywhere. She opened her mouth to say something but the words that emerged were unplanned. 'Not if I'm drinking alone...'

And there it was again...that *look*...

'Just the one, then,' Zac murmured. 'It's not my night on call but...you never know what might happen, do you?'

Olivia didn't say anything. She couldn't. That lilt in his voice seemed to be a lot more noticeable when he spoke softly and it tickled her ears deliciously. The innuendo in his words had also been more than enough to silence her. He wasn't really talking about potential medical emergencies, was he?

The atmosphere in this room suddenly felt different—as if all her senses were strangely heightened. Olivia watched the rich red of the wine tumbling into the clear glass. She could hear the gurgle of the liquid but she could also hear the sound of Zac's breath. She caught the faint waft of Chloe coming from his clothing but, beneath that, she could catch the scent of the man himself and she could swear she was aware of the actual heat of his skin. It might very well be a mistake to stay here but there was probably nothing on earth that could have persuaded her to leave.

Oh, man. What did he think he was doing, playing with fire like this?

Was he just trying to prove to himself how in control he was? Yeah…maybe that was it. Olivia followed his lead and sat down at the old wooden kitchen table but she seemed to be avoiding looking at him for a minute by letting her gaze drift around the room, taking in copper pots hanging beneath a high shelf and the wooden rack with her clothes draped over it above the pot belly stove inside a brick chimney.

'This is nice,' she said. 'Rustic.'

'I like it,' Zac agreed. 'Reminds me a bit

of the farmhouse I grew up in. In County Cork in Ireland.'

'I thought it was an Irish accent.'

The expression in those blue eyes suggested that Olivia could quite happily sit here and just listen to him talking. And that maybe his accent wasn't the only thing she liked about him. He liked it that he had her attention like this, he realised. He liked it rather a lot.

'So what brought you all the way down under to one of New Zealand's smallest towns?'

'I guess it was one of the few countries I hadn't been to. And I needed a change from big cities.'

'So you've travelled a lot?'

'Aye... I think I was born an adrenaline junkie. Always been on the hunt for adventure and excitement, me. It's no wonder my poor mother went grey so early.'

'What made you choose medicine for a career, then? Instead of being, oh, I don't know...a helicopter pilot?'

'You'd be surprised how often doctors get to go in helicopters. Especially if they put their hand up to work in war zones. Or as part of a trauma team in a major hospital like Chicago or Boston.'

Her eyes had widened. 'War zones? Really?'

'It was where I headed as soon as I was qualified enough. It's not something you can do forever, though. It's…tough…'

'I can't begin to imagine what it's like,' Olivia said quietly. She was holding his gaze and this time Zac could see respect in her eyes. And something more. Concern? Empathy, even? 'But that explains why you reacted so fast when that plane exploded. And why you looked so…'

'So…what?' Zac swallowed a mouthful of his wine but he didn't break the eye contact with Olivia. What had she seen? And why did she care?

'So… I don't know. Kind of haunted. As if something terrible was happening. Or had happened.'

'It's a long time ago now,' Zac said slowly. 'And I thought it was well behind me but I guess explosions don't happen that often and they're certainly a trigger for things I'd rather forget. It took me a while to get past the flashbacks.'

Olivia didn't say anything but her gaze told him that she was listening. Really listening. Maybe that was why he gave in to the impulse to tell her something he'd never told anybody. Or maybe he was just pushing some personal boundaries because he'd been rattled today but he'd coped perfectly well. Could he risk poking an old wound to see if it might actually be completely healed?

'I had an army medic friend,' he told her. 'Mia. A very good friend. More than a friend, in fact—we were planning to get married after that tour of duty. She was walking ahead of me one day and she stepped on a landmine.' He could do this, Zac realised. He could say the words and still keep enough distance. It felt like he was describing something he'd seen in a movie, perhaps. 'It took both her legs off and she died within a couple of minutes.'

About as long as it had taken for him to get to her and hold her in his arms, but even letting that thought surface seemed to be okay. There was no sense that some kind of mental dam was about to burst and drown him in emotion. He didn't dare take the final step, though, and admit that it had been his fault. That Mia wouldn't have even been there if he hadn't persuaded her to stay on until he was due to leave.

Olivia had her hand pressed against her mouth. She looked so shocked, Zac thought. How much more shocked would she be, though, if he told her that losing Mia like that had taught him to build barriers and protect himself by not caring too much? That it was even worse to get so good at keeping his distance that it was possible to witness a death—even that of a child—and feel absolutely nothing? That that had been the point at which he'd thought he might have to walk away from medicine forever.

No. He wasn't going to say anything more. He shouldn't have said anything in the first place but this was turning out to be a very strange day. He hadn't expected Olivia Donaldson to crash into his life. Or a plane to crash, for that matter. They were both in the category of once-in-a-lifetime events.

'Anyway…that was probably a lot more information than you wanted but it's part of the reason I ended up here. I needed some time out, I guess.' He wanted to change the subject now. 'I'd rather talk about *you*, Olivia Donaldson. I'm curious about why it only took a phone call for you to turn up in Cutler's Creek. And I'm wondering why your father never made a call like that years ago.'

Olivia shrugged. 'I guess you'll have to ask him that.'

'Don't you want to know?'

'I'm not sure I do. Like you, there are things I think I'd rather forget.'

'Fair enough.' Zac was still pushing away what he hadn't told Olivia about. Would he ever be able to forget holding that small, dying child and not feeling as if his heart was breaking? Not being able to feel anything at all? Needing something physical to do to distract himself, he eyed the receding level of wine in Olivia's glass. 'Top-up?'

'It is very nice wine.'

It was probably an unconscious action for Olivia to run her tongue slowly over her lower lip but Zac couldn't look away. If she looked up and caught his gaze right now and there was any hint of what he'd thought he'd seen in her eyes before, there would be no turning back. Hurriedly, he pushed back his chair and stood up, heading for the wine bottle on the kitchen bench.

It was completely dark outside now. The wind was picking up enough to rattle the glass in its pane and there was no question of Olivia driving anywhere after a second glass of wine. Knowing that they were going to be under the same roof for the night was… well… Zac looked over his shoulder, as if looking at her might give him whatever word he was searching for. But Olivia wasn't sitting at the table now. She'd brought her glass over and was standing right behind him.

For a long, long moment they simply stared at each other and it was a silent acknowledgement of an overwhelming sexual attraction. One that carried no strings whatsoever because it was highly unlikely that they would ever see each other again after tonight but one that meant something because they'd been through some things today that had given them an insight into each other that he suspected was probably hidden to anyone else in their lives. He had been able to see that Olivia was still affected by what she perceived as abandonment by her father. And Zac had just shared something incredibly personal because he knew that Olivia had so easily seen past the laid-back image that was his protective shield.

It was that feeling of connection that made Zac relinquish the tight hold he had on his self-control. If this was a mistake, he'd deal with any repercussions tomorrow because the temptation to lose himself for a brief moment in time was irresistible and he was quite sure that Olivia Donaldson wanted this as much as he did. Slowly, deliberately, he reached to take the wine glass out of her hand, put it down on the bench and turned back to her.

The ground was shifting beneath Olivia's feet.

She was falling. Tilting forward, anyway. Could just a couple of glasses of wine on an empty stomach have been enough to have an effect like that? No…this wasn't something you could find in a bottle. This was something that most people never found in a lifetime—an attraction to someone that was intense enough to be completely overwhelming. When it was coming from both sides, the collision was inevitable and there must have been an explosion of some kind because all oxygen in this room seemed to have vanished. Not that Olivia felt any need to breathe in this instant. All she could possibly need was…*this*…

The touch of Zac's lips on her own. The glide of his tongue dancing with hers. The searing warmth of his hands as they slid beneath that baggy sweatshirt. The silk of *his* skin as she let her own hands roam.

There was a moment when they could have both stopped. When they had to pause for breath and she saw Zac glance at the door and then back to her—a silent invitation to take this somewhere more comfortable. Like his bed...

'I don't...' Olivia had to pull in a new breath. She could hardly say she didn't want this and sound sincere. 'I mean, this isn't something I usually... I don't want you to think that...'

'I'm not thinking anything.' Zac's voice was a low growl. 'Except that you are amazing. That we happen to be together and will be for the night, but after that we're probably never going to see each other again, are we?'

She shook her head very slowly. She'd had a similar thought herself, although everything felt hazy now. One thing was very clear, though. She couldn't stop. The pull of desire was threatening to drown her.

Something banged overhead, as if a gust of wind had lifted a sheet of the corrugated-iron roof and then let it slam down again. The startling sound was instantly followed by the brief rattle of heavy rain and it felt like a drumbeat that was adding to the intensity of what was happening here. Olivia knew she might never feel passion like this again in her lifetime and she had to know what it would be like.

Just once…

CHAPTER FIVE

IT WAS THE rumble of distant thunder that woke Olivia the next morning.

For a minute or two she didn't open her eyes. She wanted to snuggle a little deeper beneath the soft duvet and bask in the warmth of this bed. She knew she was alone and that was okay. She could take her time to stretch her limbs just enough to wake up her muscles and skin. To let her mind drift and sift through the memories of a night she was never going to forget.

A sexual fantasy that she'd made the most of because she knew it was never going to happen again. She'd had no idea that sex could ever be that good. That someone could tease her to the brink of something so huge, hold her there until she was begging for release and then take her even further before letting her fall off the edge of bliss. And the things she'd wanted to do to him… She'd never imagined that she could feel comfortable enough with anyone to be so uninhibited. She could actually feel herself blushing a little as she remembered.

Okay…maybe that was enough sifting for now. Olivia opened her eyes and moved to get herself up. It was no real surprise that she'd slept through Zac leaving this bed. He'd warned her that he would probably be gone by the time she woke up and she'd been deeply asleep because it can't have been very long ago that they'd finally found themselves too sated to begin making love yet again. She could feel her still-weary body protesting as she pulled the duvet with her to use as a cover when she rolled out of bed. What time was it? She had to get on the road and drive to the airport. She had to leave this fantasy behind and head straight back into her real life.

'Zac?'

Her call echoed down the hallway of the

cottage and Olivia knew that he was gone. It wasn't simply because there was no response, it was because the air felt flat. The charged atmosphere that their mutual attraction had created was merely a memory. Like a fragment of a dream that had no relevance in real life. Padding through the house in her bare feet after a quick shower, Olivia retrieved her clothes from the rack above the stove in the kitchen. They were going to look appalling and that rip in her skirt was barely decent but it couldn't be helped.

There had to be some shop at the airport where she could purchase something else to travel in. She didn't have her hair straightener with her so it wasn't possible to give her hair its normal sleek look but she twisted it into a loose braid that would, at least, keep it out of her face. Thank goodness she always carried a basic makeup kit in her large shoulder bag.

The kitchen was a bit of a mess. She'd almost forgotten that they'd found themselves starving in the earliest hours of the new day and had come in here to make fried-egg sandwiches with thick slices of bread and a layer of onion jam. She'd been wearing nothing but Zac's T-shirt that was big enough to be almost decent. He'd been wearing the tracksuit pants that she'd borrowed earlier. They'd polished off that bottle of wine, too, and it had been the most delicious meal Olivia had ever eaten. Should she take the time to wash the frying pan and plates that were cluttering the sink now and give herself the luxury of sinking into the memory of that meal and what had happened again as soon as they'd finished it?

No. She might still have plenty of time to get to the airport but she needed to allow extra to drive as carefully as possible through that gorge. Especially with the weather still deteriorating. There had been intermittent rain squalls during the night but apparently there was a real storm on the way and that rumble of thunder that had woken Olivia had been a warning that it was nearly here. Through the window above the sink, she looked up at an ominous steel-grey sky where billowing clouds had an eerie light to their edges. A flicker of lightning near the mountains made her turn away. The sooner she hit the road, the better.

But… Her head swung back as what she'd caught in her peripheral vision registered. Yes. The gate to that paddock beyond the garden hedge was open. And… Olivia leaned over the sink to see more and her heart sank. Yes…there was Chloe the horse, standing to one side of a vegetable garden. She might not have any obligation to deal with dirty dishes before she left Zac's house but she couldn't leave his horse somewhere unsafe. What if she got out onto the road and was hit by a truck?

Olivia found the last of the carrots in the fridge in case she needed an incentive to persuade Chloe to return to her paddock but when she went out the back door into the garden there was no nicker of appreciation for any treats. Chloe's head was hanging low and she had a strangely hunched look to her back. By the time Olivia had walked the short distance to reach the horse, Chloe had crumpled to the ground and was stretched out flat on her side.

'Oh, my God...' Olivia crouched by Chloe's huge head. 'What's wrong?' She patted her neck. 'Don't worry. I'll go and call Zac. He'll know what to do.'

She didn't have his phone number, she realised as she ran back into the house, but she could look up contact details for the hospital and get hold of him that way. Except that as she was searching online, the power on her phone died and it was at that point that she remembered that she'd hadn't thought it was necessary to bring her charger. Because she'd expected to be back in Auckland well before it was needed.

This was turning into a nightmare. Could she leave Chloe and drive to the hospital to find Zac? Olivia took a deep breath and went out to see if anything had changed. The horse was still lying on its side and Olivia could hear loud grunting noises. She could also see what looked like a white balloon expanding under Chloe's tail. It took only seconds to realise what was happening. The pregnancy *had* been genuine and Chloe's baby was about to be born. Had the mare broken through that wooden gate looking for help as her contractions started? Olivia crouched to stroke Chloe's neck again.

'It's okay,' she told the horse. 'You're going to be fine. I'll be here to help.'

She had to be. However long this took and however difficult any consequences might be, there was no way Olivia could drive away now. She had to wait to make sure the foal arrived safely and she would also have to get them both into shelter, preferably before this storm broke. Leaving Chloe for a few minutes, she went to check the barn to one side of the cottage and was relieved to find it empty apart from a water trough in a penned-off area and a stack of bales, both straw and hay. Pulling the twine from a bale of straw, she scattered it over the cobbled floor of the pen. Then it was back to Chloe to find that the balloon now contained the front hooves and the head of the foal pressed against the legs.

'You're doing so well,' she told Chloe. 'Keep going... Big push...'

The mare's grunts and groans sounded almost human and the whole of her enormous body was moving with the intensity of her contractions. Olivia had no idea how long she was there, trying to encourage and reassure Chloe with her voice and touch as she watched what was happening. Was it too slow? What was she going to do if a vet was needed? Finally, with an even bigger contraction, the foal's body slid onto the ground, still encased in that thick white membrane.

Olivia knew what she needed to do now. She stepped around Chloe's huge, fluffy feet to reach the foal and she broke the membrane and pulled it back so that the baby could take its first breath. Chloe lifted her head and then curled her front legs in and pushed herself to her feet, breaking the umbilical cord as she did so. She came to sniff the foal cautiously as Olivia pulled more of the membrane away. The foal tried but failed to lift its head. It would be some time before it was strong enough to be on its feet, Olivia realised, and she didn't need the chill of a wind gust bringing a splatter of rain to remind her that she couldn't leave either of these animals out in this weather.

The foal was not small and it took an enormous effort for Olivia to lift and then half carry, half drag it to safety. At least Chloe didn't object to her intervention and followed her into the barn. There, Olivia could start rubbing the foal with handfuls of straw and its mother started to lick its face thoroughly. The foal made a stronger effort to move and managed to keep its head up this time.

'There you go...' She could feel a smile that just kept getting wider, but oddly she had tears on her face at the same time. 'You know what to do, don't you, Chloe? And look...isn't your baby just gorgeous?'

Having made sure the water trough was full, Olivia stood for several minutes and watched the mother and baby get to know each other and the foal make new attempts to get to its feet. It was adorably wobbly but the determination was there and it wouldn't be long before it could get the milk it needed. Long enough for Olivia to go back into the house and change her clothes. Her suit was really ruined this time, so she had no choice but to get back into the clothes Zac had provided yesterday.

She also had no choice but to drive back into Cutler's Creek when she was finally satisfied that the animals were safe. She might have vowed never to set foot in this community hospital again but Zac needed to know about the new arrival. It was only going to add an extra twenty minutes to her journey and, with a bit of luck, she might actually still get to the airport in time.

Or perhaps a lot of luck. The flash of lightning as she turned her car onto the road was almost blinding and the crack of thunder followed so fast she knew that the storm was right on top of them. Even with her windscreen wipers on the highest speed, visibility was poor in the torrential rain that began only minutes later.

Olivia could only grit her teeth and keep going. What was it about this place? Nobody was going to believe the series of extraordinary events the last twenty-four hours had provided. On the plus side, it would make for entertaining dinner-party conversations in years to come, wouldn't it? Being first on the scene at a plane crash. Delivering a Clydesdale horse's foal. Driving through an apocalyptic storm. Fantasy sex with the most gorgeous man in existence...

No. That could never come up in conversation with anyone.

It was something totally private that belonged only to her. And Isaac Cameron.

'Look at that, baby George.' Zac held Faye Morris's two-day-old baby up to the window. 'That's one heck of a storm you're going to go home in.'

He turned back to where Faye was packing her small suitcase. Debbie, her midwife, was folding some baby clothes. 'You sure you don't want to wait it out?'

He wondered if Olivia had got past the gorge already on her journey north. He hoped so because it would be a tricky drive in conditions like this and he certainly wouldn't want her involved in any kind of accident.

'I'd rather be at home on the farm,' Faye said. 'With our log burner going full tilt and a pot of soup on the stove. Besides, George's older brother is running his father ragged. Jamie's hit the "terrible twos" with a flying start.' She came to look out of the window and had to grimace. 'It does look a bit nasty. We'll have to make a dash for the truck.' She rubbed at where her breath had misted up the glass. 'Speaking of dashing…who's that coming in so fast?'

Zac could feel the hairs on the back of his neck prickle. Nobody skidded to a halt like that outside the doors of a hospital unless someone was in trouble. He pressed the bundle of baby he was holding back into Faye's arms and headed out of her room at a near run, with Debbie hot on his heels. He got to the main reception area at the same time the occupants of the car came through the doors but he had been able to hear screams from the other end of the corridor.

He knew the tall man who was carrying the screaming girl. Mike was one of the local firemen who'd been at the crash scene yesterday. It had to be his youngest daughter he had in his arms and she was clutching at a blood-soaked towel wrapped around her head and face.

'Come this way, Mike…' Zac led the way to their minor procedures room, which doubled as their emergency department. 'What's happened?'

'Shayna was heading out to catch the school bus. She got hit by a piece of iron. Must've come off one of the dog kennels in that wind, I reckon.'

Debbie was still right behind him. 'What do you need, Zac?'

'A dressing kit for now, thanks. And saline.'

Sixteen-year-old Shayna was still screaming as Zac helped Mike to put her on the bed. 'It's okay, Shayna,' he said. 'We're going to look after you. Try and take a deep breath for me and calm down. I need you to tell me what's happening for you.' He glanced up at her father. 'Was she knocked out?'

'Don't think so. Knocked over, but I saw her from the house and she got straight back up. Came in with blood pouring everywhere so I grabbed the first clean thing I could find to put some pressure on the cut.'

'Good job.' Zac was easing the towel away from Shayna's head. 'The bleeding's stopped, which is great.' What wasn't great was that it was a deep wound that had carved out a V of flesh that was hanging just above Shayna's eye.

'It's my eye,' Shayna sobbed. 'I'm blind...'

Carefully, Zac lifted the flap of skin and held a sterile gauze pad over it to keep it in place. Although the eyebrow was involved, her eyelid seemed to be uninjured.

'You've got your eyes closed, sweetheart,' he told Shayna. 'I think you'll find you can see if you open them.'

'I can't. They'll be all full of blood.'

'I promise they won't be. Look, I'm going to put a bandage around to keep this dressing in place and make sure it doesn't start bleeding again. And then we're going to check you out properly.'

A thorough neurological check came next, along with making sure there were no other injuries that had been missed. He took Mike out of the room to talk to him while Debbie began to sponge dried blood off the girl's face and hands.

'She's okay,' he told the worried father. 'It's a deep laceration but there's no evidence of an underlying head injury or nerve damage, which is good news.'

'She'll need stitches, though, won't she?'

'Yes. The wound is too large and deep not to be stitched and, because it's on her face, it needs to be done by an expert to minimise scarring. I'm thinking we should transfer her to Dunedin and get a referral to a plastic surgeon.'

Plastic surgeon… How many times was he going to be thinking about Olivia Donaldson today? Even as he pushed that awareness out of his mind, he could feel the tingle of sensation that ran through his limbs to pool somewhere deep in his belly.

Man, that had been a night to remember last night, hadn't it?

'She won't be going anywhere in a hurry,' Mike told him. 'Nobody will be flying in this and Bruce is even thinking of closing the gorge road. That wind is getting dangerous. I was already getting calls to the station for things like roof damage before I brought Shayna in. Which reminds me…reception is lousy at the moment with this weather, and I need to let them know where I am. Where's your nearest landline?'

'Reception. Come with me.'

He might need to make some calls himself,

Zac decided. To bring in some extra staff because it looked as though Cutler's Creek was in for a rough day. How many other storm-related injuries could come in?

'Where's Don, Jill?' he asked the receptionist as Mike called the fire station.

'On his way. He had to go and check that his mother was okay. Some windows of her house blew in. Oh...' She turned her head. 'That's probably him arriving now.'

Except it wasn't.

It was his daughter and, if anything, Olivia Donaldson looked more of a mess than she had in the wake of helping with that accident scene yesterday. There were strands of hair that had escaped from a plait and glued themselves to her face. She was streaked with what looked like mud and... Why was she still wearing his clothes?

'It's your horse,' she told Zac. 'Chloe. She's just had her baby...'

'No way...' He knew he was staring. Not at how dishevelled she was or the dirt she had on her face. He was holding those extraordinary eyes because it was hard not to feel like they were the only two people in this space. In the world, even, for just a heartbeat. 'Is… is everything okay?'

Olivia nodded. Smiled, in fact. 'I stayed with her. I got them both into the barn and there's clean straw and hay and water. I just thought you should know. And…and my phone had died.' She looked at Mike, who was still using the phone on the reception desk. 'I don't suppose I could use your landline? I need to check the status of my flight.'

Mike put the phone down. He'd overheard Olivia's last comment. 'Dunedin airport is closed,' he told her. 'So's Queenstown. And Invercargill. You won't be driving anywhere, either, because the police have just closed the gorge road. There's been a slip.'

'But… I *have* to… I can't stay here.'

Zac saw the way Olivia's gaze raked the area—as if she was afraid she might see her father again at any moment. It was just as well the person coming in from the corridor was Debbie.

'Shayna's asking for you,' she told Mike. 'And she wants to know when her mum is getting here.' Her voice trailed off as she stared at Olivia.

Everybody was staring at Olivia and Zac felt the sudden need to protect her. Of course she didn't want to be here. He'd had the privilege of getting to know this woman on a very intimate level last night and he knew that she was a very different person from the one he'd thought he'd been leaving that voicemail for. Olivia Donaldson had an intelligence to match her beauty and she was passionate and generous but had an edge of vulnerability that he guessed had its roots in what must have been a difficult childhood. He'd been judgemental without knowing the truth. He owed her more than an apology for his assumptions.

He stepped closer to Olivia and caught her gaze, trying to convey the silent message that he was going to make this awkward situation better for her if it was at all possible. Then he turned to the other people around them.

'This is Olivia Donaldson,' he told them. 'Another Dr Donaldson—and, yes, she's our Dr Donaldson's daughter but that's none of our business. Through no fault of her own, she's stuck here until the road's open again so let's make her feel welcome. Debbie, perhaps you could find Olivia a set of scrubs, please?'

'Of course. Come with me, Dr Donaldson.'

Zac lowered his voice as he leaned closer to Olivia. 'Sorry about this but there's really nothing we can do other than make the best of it, yes?'

As if to applaud his attitude, there was another huge crack of thunder outside and then the lights flickered and went out around them. Even though it was daytime, it felt as if they'd been plunged into late evening.

'Oh, no… Shayna…' Debbie turned towards the doors. 'I'd better get back to her.'

'It's okay,' Zac said. 'The generator will kick in very soon.'

Mike looked torn. 'I need to get to the fire

station,' he said. 'But I don't want to leave Shayna until her mum gets here.'

'We'll look after her,' Zac promised. 'And you know what? It's actually a real stroke of luck that Dr Donaldson's been trapped here with us.'

'Why's that?' Mike sounded even more suspicious than Olivia was looking.

'Olivia's a plastic surgeon,' Zac told him. 'She has the perfect qualifications to tell us the best way to manage Shayna's injury.' He turned back to Olivia. 'We've got a young girl with a serious facial laceration,' he explained. 'Could I trouble you for a specialist consultation, please?'

He liked the way he could see Olivia straighten her back. She was standing in possibly the last place in the world she wanted to be and she was being forced to stay here by circumstances that she couldn't possibly control. She was also dishevelled and dirty, which was obviously not the way she would want to present herself anywhere, but here she was drawing on some inner strength and turning into a professional person before his very eyes. A person who was confident of the skills she might have to offer. Proud of them, in fact.

'Certainly, Dr Cameron.' She nodded. 'Just show me where to find those scrubs and give me five minutes to clean up.'

Zac's smile of appreciation barely had time to touch his lips before the front doors of the hospital slid open beside them to let in a blast of icy wind and rain.

'Oh…no…' Olivia's barely audible reaction was so heartfelt that Zac took a step closer. As he turned, he could feel his shoulder touching Olivia's and it felt as if she was glad of the contact. As if she was leaning closer rather than moving away.

Her father had just come in, his arm supporting a much older woman. The umbrella he had in his hand had turned inside out and he looked windblown and damp. He also looked completely shocked to see Olivia.

'You're still *here*?'

Zac could feel the tension in Olivia's body

increase and it felt like she was still tapping into whatever professional mode she had accessed when he'd asked her for a consultation. She intended to cope with this situation, no matter how difficult it might be, and Zac... Well, he was proud of her, that's what he was.

The older woman was small and plump. She peered over her glasses at the people in front of her.

'Well...' she said. 'This is a turn-up for the books, isn't it?' She nodded at Zac. 'Don insisted I come in with him,' she apologised. 'I had a bit of a fall, trying to get away from my broken window. He seems to think I might need an X-ray of my wrist.'

Olivia's father had an odd look on his face. It was obvious that Olivia was the last person he had expected—or *wanted*—to see but he didn't look angry. He looked nervous, she thought. Scared, even?

'No problem, Mabel,' Zac said. 'I'll look after that for you very soon.'

She gave him a bright smile and then turned her head, her gaze zeroing in on Olivia with such focus it sent a shiver down her spine.

'You must be Olivia,' she said. 'I heard you'd been in town and I'm so happy you haven't left just yet.'

'Oh?' Olivia felt an urge to step back as the elderly woman walked towards her but she found she couldn't move. There were creases in this Mabel's face that had nothing to do with age lines. They suggested a warmth that came from smiling often and they deepened visibly as she smiled at Olivia. She really was happy to see her.

'I'm Mabel Donaldson. I'm your grandmother.'

CHAPTER SIX

THE LIGHTS FLICKERED back into life around them as Mabel Donaldson reached up to touch Olivia's cheek.

'I can't tell you how thrilled I am to meet you, darling. And I can't wait for us to have a proper chat.'

It was a total surprise to find she had another member of her family in Cutler's Creek. Her grandfather had died so long ago that it hadn't occurred to Olivia that his wife might still be here decades later. To feel as if finally meeting her was the best thing that could have happened for her grandmother was just as astonishing. Nobody had ever called Olivia "darling". Not her parents. Not even Patrick.

The phone on Jill's desk was ringing. 'Cutler's Creek Community Hospital,' she said when she answered the call. 'How can I help you?' She held out the phone a few seconds later.

'It's for you, Dr Donaldson,' she said.

Don Donaldson moved towards the desk but Jill shook her head. 'No...the other Dr Donaldson. It's someone called Simon Ellis.'

'Who the heck is Simon Ellis?' Zac asked.

Olivia swallowed. 'My boss.' She was a little nervous about speaking to Simon. She suspected he would have been disappointed that she'd chosen not to go to that gala. Now she had to tell him that she wasn't even going to be at work anytime soon. But he didn't sound angry.

'Thank goodness you're all right,' he said. 'I've been trying to call you all morning.'

'Sorry. I didn't bring my charger. I wasn't expecting to have to stay but there was an accident—'

'I know... I saw you on the news. Way to go, Olivia. I've made sure that the media knows you're employed by the Plastic Surgery Institute. It's great publicity for us. Plastic surgeons are *real* doctors, too. Pure gold.'

Olivia could hear an approving smile in his voice but found it disturbing. Would he be so happy if she hadn't inadvertently given the private clinic some free publicity? Having a spotlight on her that was better than being seen at some charity event?

'I'm stuck here now because of the storm,' she told him. 'The airports are closed. So's the road.'

'Don't worry about a thing. We've got all your patients covered. It's not a problem.'

'Thanks, Simon. I appreciate that.'

People were moving around her. Mike the fireman was leaving, going out the front doors. Her father and grandmother were heading in the opposite direction, into the hospital—the direction that the nurse, Debbie, had taken when the power had cut out. Zac was still here, though. Watching her. She could feel that gaze on her skin like a physical touch...

'I've got to go,' she said. 'I've got a patient waiting for me.'

'What? You don't need to go overboard, you know. Don't take on something that might turn into a problem.'

And cause adverse publicity? Olivia gave her head a tiny shake. 'I'll be in touch, Simon, when I know where I am.'

Zac had clearly been waiting for her to finish the call. 'I'll show you our storage area and bathroom,' he said. 'And where to find me when you're ready for action.'

His smile was barely there but Olivia could feel a warmth that felt almost as welcoming as her grandmother's and that lilt in his voice seemed even more charming after listening to Simon's crisply enunciated vowels. She actually wanted to be here, Olivia realised as she changed into the scrubs Zac had provided and used the bathroom facilities to clean up and tidy her hair. Much more than she wanted to be in Auckland. And, okay, she wouldn't have chosen to be here and her father certainly wasn't happy that she hadn't disappeared yet but… Zac wanted her to be here. Plus, she had a grandmother who had been genuinely delighted to see her.

Who had called her "darling".

It wasn't just how long the storm would take to blow over that would enable Olivia to tell Simon where she was in terms of returning to her work and her normal life. It felt like the foundations of her world were still shifting beneath her feet and this time she couldn't run away. She would have to face everything head on. Starting with a young girl who might need her help if she wasn't going to end up being scarred for life. She had been shown the direction to take to find the minor procedures room but Olivia found an obstacle around the first corner.

A human obstacle.

And her father still looked, inexplicably, nervous.

'Ah… Lib—Olivia. Could I have a word?'

He was standing right in front of her. She could step around him, given that there was no one else in sight, but Olivia's feet had stopped without any conscious direction.

'I...um... I think I should apologise. I was rather rude yesterday.'

Olivia couldn't argue with that. She said nothing and, for a long moment, they simply stared at each other.

Don cleared his throat. 'I didn't expect you to still be here.'

'No. I didn't expect it, either.' That feeling of having old wounds opened up increased. 'Don't worry, I'll be leaving as soon as I can.'

'My mother...your grandmother is going to want to talk to you.'

'So it seems.' And part of Olivia wanted that. She hadn't had any grandparents on her mother's side. Or not that she knew of, but there were doubts waiting to surface about all sorts of things concerning her mother now, weren't there?

'She doesn't know.' There was an urgent note in her father's voice. 'About me. About...

about the cancer and…and I'd be grateful if you didn't say anything.'

Olivia could feel her jaw dropping. He wasn't going to tell his own mother that he was dying?

'It's just that it's her ninetieth birthday in a couple of weeks. The whole community is planning to celebrate and I really don't want to spoil that for her. I'll tell her afterwards but…it would be better for everybody if that party wasn't spoiled in any way.'

At least he cared about his mother, Olivia thought, but she could feel a wash of bitterness lacing itself into the pain of those old wounds.

'As you said yourself,' she muttered, 'it's not really any of my business, is it?' But it felt like it was. Or that she wanted it to be.

'Thank you. And I…' He seemed to catch his breath as a look of pain crossed his face. 'I'm…sorry. For everything.'

Was that physical or emotional pain he was experiencing? It certainly looked real and Olivia felt a beat of concern. But that apology?

'You think that makes everything all right? That you can just say sorry for everything you did? Or should that be everything you *didn't* do?'

'You don't know what I tried—and unfortunately failed—to do.'

'I know that you failed to be a good husband. Or a good father.'

'Marriages fail, Olivia. Sometimes people just want different things from life. And they want them so badly that they are prepared to hurt others to make sure they get what they want.'

'What are you talking about? That you wanted to come back here so much that your family didn't matter any more?'

'I was always going to come back here. Your mother said she was happy about that but she was a city girl through and through and she had no idea what she was signing up for. In the end, she couldn't do it. And she wasn't going to let you be taken to live in a place like this. She said it had nothing to offer you and she was going to make sure you only got the best of everything.'

Olivia had to brush away an echo of that memory of her mother telling her that Cutler's Creek didn't even have a proper school. And Zac's voice telling her that she was such a city girl, but he didn't know her, did he? She hadn't thought of herself as being like her mother and she was less sure than she had been, even a day or two ago, that she wanted to be focused on her career more than anything else in life.

But surely that wasn't entirely her mother's fault?

'You couldn't make the effort to stay in touch,' she accused her father. 'Have you any idea what that was like for *me*?'

Again, Don closed his eyes tightly and seemed to be holding his breath, waiting for a wave of pain to pass. When he spoke, his voice was ragged. 'I know an apology will never be enough but that's all I've got to offer.'

No. It could never be enough. Except that Olivia's gaze was locked on her father's face. On dark blue eyes that were a mirror image of her own and she could see something very genuine in those eyes. Worse, she caught a whiff of the aftershave he was wearing and it was like she'd stepped into a time machine. She hadn't invented those memories of what her father had once been like. They were all real and she was a child again and all she wanted to do was hurl herself into her daddy's arms and feel them folding her into a bear hug. She *wanted* that apology to be enough. For there to be a way back...

'Liv?'

Zac's call was more than welcome. It offered an escape from a confusion that Olivia didn't want anything to do with. She could even forgive him for using the short version of her name that her friends used because, right now, he felt like a friend. He was rescuing her from the emotional minefield that being with her father represented.

'I'm ready.' Olivia turned her back on her

father and moved swiftly. 'Let's see what we've got and whether there's anything I can do to help.'

It was an enormous relief to have something clinical to focus on and satisfying to know that she had the skills to make a real difference. Zac took her aside to discuss the case after her assessment, leaving Debbie keeping Shayna company for a minute. Debbie was also a midwife, Olivia had learned, and both she and Shayna had been easy to find a rapport with as she'd told them all about the foal's delivery while she had examined her patient carefully.

'So what do you think?' Zac was trusting her judgement here. That felt good, too.

'The frontal branch of the facial nerve is intact but it's a deep wound and the capillary refill at the edges isn't great. If it's just stitched as it is, it could leave a scar that will need more surgery in the future.'

'Can you manage it?'

'Of course, but how well I can do depends what you've got available. A magnifying headset with a light? Good range of sutures and surgical instruments?'

'Yes. I'm sure we have everything you could need. Your dad has always had enormous community support to ensure we're very well equipped.'

'I can use a supraorbital nerve block for anaesthesia without the tissue distortion that injecting local could create but, given how anxious Shayna is, I think she'll need a good level of sedation. Ideally, I'd want to do this under a general anaesthetic but I don't suppose that's an option here?'

'We do actually have an operating theatre and all the gear but it's been many years since it was used. It would have to be a life-or-death emergency to justify the risk.'

'Sedation it is, then. But I'll need you to monitor her.'

'I'm all yours.' Zac's smile was warm. 'Thanks, Liv. I really appreciate this.'

This time, the short version of her name sounded perfectly natural coming from Zac. As if they'd been friends forever. His smile felt equally familiar and it had the effect of making something deep inside Olivia feel like it was melting.

But she couldn't allow herself to acknowledge that reaction, let alone wonder what it meant. She had a job to do. Zac might have been in charge at the accident scene yesterday but the spotlight was firmly on her this time and she was going to do her absolute best.

For Shayna.

And for Zac.

Wow…

Just wow…

Zac had been watching Olivia Donaldson very closely for some minutes and he was blown away by her skills. And her confidence. He was learning stuff here. They were alone in the room with Shayna because her mother had arrived and Debbie had gone to make her a cup of tea and keep her company while the stitching was being done.

'See that blue tinge?' She had pressed the

edges of the wound with a haemostat. 'No capillary refill. That tissue's not going to make it.'

'What's the answer? To trim the edges first?'

'Trick I learned years ago. Watch this.'

Olivia picked up a suture from the sterile tray she had prepared while Zac had been putting an IV line into Shayna's arm and giving her the drugs that would keep her asleep for a short time.

'I'm putting in a whip stitch, taking the smallest possible bites to bring the edges together. You don't even think about trimming, or what's going on with the deeper structures.' Then she reached for a scalpel. 'Now I'm going to cut down one side of the stitch and then the other.'

Her hands were absolutely steady as she made cuts so close together they almost looked as if they were in the same line, but then she picked up the line of suture material with forceps and lifted it clear.

'See that? Nice, smooth, healthy edges to

put together, which will give us better clo-sure and therefore a better scar. Now we do the deep dermal tissue absorbable sutures.'

She worked at an impressive speed, the curved needle taking a bite from one side of the wound and then the other, the knot being tied so fast it would have been impossible to see what she was doing if he didn't know the procedure so well himself.

'You're good,' Zac murmured. 'And I know. I've done my fair share of stitching over the years.'

'I love it. I've still got room to improve, though. With some more postgraduate train-ing I might be able to do more reconstructive work. The kind that can make a real differ-ence to people's lives.'

'That's what you want to do?'

'It's something I'm definitely interested in. I certainly want to do more than appearance medicine, anyway.'

So she wasn't just a private cosmetic sur-geon pandering to people wealthy enough to change their appearance. But he'd known that already, hadn't he? He felt like he knew a lot about this woman, even though she hadn't intentionally revealed it. Like that look of being totally lost on her face when he'd found her talking to her father earlier. Then she'd looked genuinely pleased to see *him* and he'd felt something he hadn't felt in…well, it felt like forever. Since Mia, and that was years ago now. A need to be with someone. A desire to be as close as possible to that someone. And an urge to do whatever it might take to achieve that.

The kind of feeling that meant you cared. A lot. The kind of feeling that, if it was allowed to grow, could mean that even falling in love was a possibility. In a way, it was a relief to know that he was still capable of feeling like that about someone if he chose to let it happen but, on the other hand, it was a warning that couldn't be ignored. Get involved and you got hurt. Get hurt often enough and you lose faith in humanity and even in yourself.

It was much safer being a lone wolf and

Zac knew exactly how to respond to that warning because he'd done it often enough in recent years. You moved on. You found new places to roam and people who were no more than strangers. Where you could care enough to make sure that you provided the best possible medical care but you never crossed that line.

You never got so close to someone that you simply wanted to be there. To watch them breathe…

'Almost done,' Olivia murmured. Shayna made a tiny sound that could have been expressing relief and Olivia smiled. 'It looks like the sedation is wearing off. That's good timing.'

'It is. What do you need for a dressing?'

'Some antibiotic cream and just some dry gauze for the first day. She can look after herself after that, washing it with gentle soap and water. She'll need to sleep with an extra pillow for a few days and avoid any bending or heavy lifting. I'll have a chat to her mother about that.'

'I'll send her in. I need to go and do that X-ray of your grandmother's wrist. I hope she's not going to be in a cast for her birthday party.' Zac was watching Olivia's face closely as she cut her last suture. How did she feel about that chance meeting? 'It might make her dangerous on the dance floor.'

Yes…he could see the flicker of surprise—or possibly interest—in the way her gaze flicked up to meet his. And then he could see the shutters come down. She didn't want to talk about her estranged family.

It was safe to leave Shayna now, as the sedation wore off. 'I'll ask Debbie to show you where the staffroom is,' Zac added. 'Help yourself to some coffee and biscuits. You never know, I might need your help again before we're out of this storm.'

You never know.

It seemed to be a favourite thing for Isaac Cameron to say. He'd said he would only have one glass of wine last night because you never knew what might happen.

Well…they knew now…

And Olivia couldn't stop thinking about it, especially after she'd been sitting in this empty staffroom for over an hour. Every crack of thunder that made this old wooden building vibrate seemed to reignite the tingling in every cell of her body that still hadn't worn off. She'd known that it might well be a once-in-a-lifetime experience and she'd been fine with that so why did it now feel like nothing else was ever going to get close enough to make it seem worthwhile or even desirable?

It was bad enough that it was so easy to remember every touch from Zac. Every kiss. The tenderness that had gone hand in hand with that unbelievable passion. That instead of being an experience that she could file away as a magic memory, which was what had been intended, Olivia couldn't deny that the desire to do it again was unexpectedly strong. Or that when Zac walked into the staffroom and smiled at her, it was fierce enough to make it feel like her heart stopped for a moment. Her breathing certainly did. Or maybe there just wasn't enough oxygen in here, like that lack she'd noticed in his kitchen last night.

'That's some storm out there, isn't it?'

'Mmm…' Olivia's response sounded a bit strangled but Zac didn't seem to notice. He was helping himself to coffee from the cafetière.

'Your grandma's wrist is only sprained.'

'Oh…that's good.'

'I should warn you that she's planning to give you an invitation to her birthday party. She's insisted on being taken home to fetch one, along with something else she wants to show you but I have no idea what that might be.'

Olivia shrugged. 'I doubt very much that I'll be coming back here anytime soon for a party. Coming back ever, for that matter.'

Zac turned to face Olivia, his coffee mug in his hands. 'Funny… Apparently that's pretty much what your mother said the only time she ever came here.' His breath came out in a soft snort. 'Mabel's been telling me all about her. She said, "And she always got what she wanted, that one. I've never met anyone so driven."'

'I don't need to hear the local gossip about my mother, thanks very much.'

Zac's gaze was steady. 'Even if it explains why your father gave up trying to contact you?'

Olivia was silent. She couldn't look away. Her voice came out as a whisper. 'What are you talking about?'

'Your parents agreed to separate. Your dad had to come back here to help his father or the hospital would have been closed. He didn't agree to you being taken out of the country but that's what your mother did and then she used lawyers to make it impossible for him to get access unless he wanted a huge legal battle. He tried ringing but your mother wouldn't let him talk to you. She said you were having enough trouble settling in a new place and that if he cared about you, he would wait. So he waited. And waited. He sent you cards and letters and gifts but they all got sent back, and every time it broke his heart. And then you finally sent *him* a letter—asking him never to contact you again.'

Olivia closed her eyes for a long moment. She could remember having that "trouble settling" only too well. So many tears because she'd missed her father so much.

Had her mother been so "driven" that she'd really believed that she was setting up the best future she could for her daughter by making sure nothing would hold her back from success and a stellar career? Had she sent those letters and parcels back so as not to have her message diluted?

Olivia could remember sending that letter to her father, too, with her mother helping her with the wording. She could remember how angry she'd been because it had been easier to cope with anger than any more grief. It had made her feel as if she was in control finally. That she could not let it affect her life any more than it already had.

'You okay?'

She hadn't realised that Zac had put his mug down and come towards her. Or that she had put her head in her hands because of the way it was spinning. The way Zac took her hand in his and then put his other hand over the top of it had the effect of stopping that spinning. It felt like an anchor.

She looked up. 'Do you believe that?'

'I only know what I've seen. That your grandmother was perfectly sincere and she's not actually one to gossip. And that your father *was* crying when he was looking at those old letters.'

Olivia swallowed hard. Her mother had been at the top of her field. Ambitious. Success had always been the yardstick of acceptability and the only way Olivia could find the approval that made it feel as though she was loved.

'Even if it is true,' she muttered finally, 'it's too late. It can't change anything.'

'No?' Zac gave her hand a squeeze and then let go. 'He's not a bad man, your dad,

Liv. Quite the opposite. Sometimes…' His breath came out in a sigh this time. 'Sometimes you have to shut yourself off from something that hurts too much because, if you don't, it can destroy you. It *will* destroy you.'

He went to pick up his mug of coffee but he didn't drink any more of it. He took it to the sink and emptied it out. Then he turned on the tap to rinse it.

Olivia was staring at his back. He'd sounded as if he knew what he was talking about. As if he'd had to do exactly that and shut himself off because something had hurt him too much. Her hand felt cold now that it was no longer between Zac's. She wanted that touch again. She wanted to somehow help him get past the things that haunted him. How heartbreaking must it have been for him to lose the woman he loved in such a horrific way? And he'd said that Mia's death was only part of the reason he'd come to the most isolated part of the world he could find. How much else had Zac had to deal with?

He'd mentioned flashbacks. It would be no surprise that the traumatic things he'd witnessed had affected him badly.

She wanted to walk over to him and wrap her arms around him. To tell him that she understood. She wanted to tell him that she cared. That she wanted, if it was at all possible, to make it better for him somehow. The power of how much she wanted all those things stole her breath away.

How could you feel that strongly about someone who'd been a complete stranger only twenty-four hours ago? But the thought of Zac being a stranger was also weird. It was as if she'd been unknowingly searching for something for her entire life and she had finally found it. No—not some*thing*. Some-*one*.

But Oliva didn't believe in soul mates. Or love at first sight. Because they were based on emotional reactions that couldn't be trusted to last. Like you couldn't trust that the people you loved the most were actually going to stay in your life. Over-the-top emotions were not acceptable because they messed with your head and made you vulnerable. Like Zac had just said himself, if you cared too much, it could destroy you.

For a heartbeat, Olivia felt something like fear. That something important could be in imminent danger of being destroyed?

Did she care too much already? Fate was forcing her to stay in a place where there was a pull that seemed to be dragging her in. A pull towards a past where she'd had a father she'd adored who'd loved her just as much. Towards a grandmother she'd never met but who seemed ready to welcome her with open arms.

Towards an extraordinary man that—just maybe—she'd been waiting her entire life to meet?

CHAPTER SEVEN

THE STORM CONTINUED to batter the small town of Cutler's Creek.

Mabel Donaldson had not yet arrived back at the hospital with whatever it was she wanted to show Olivia but a lunch of toasted cheese sandwiches and a delicious vegetable soup was being provided by a lovely woman called Betty who was in charge of the hospital's kitchen and laundry. Everybody seemed to be welcome in her kitchen, whether they worked in this hospital or not, and they all seemed to know when lunch was being served.

Zac came in and announced to no one in particular that he'd finished a check on all the inpatients and that they were now all enjoying their lunch. He happily accepted a large mug of soup from Betty and helped himself to a sandwich from the pile on the platter.

Bruce, the local police officer, arrived. 'I went past your place a while ago,' he told Zac. 'Your roof's still on and the barn's secure. Just as well that foal's out of the weather, that's for sure.'

'Thanks to Liv,' Zac told him.

'Didn't realise you'd stayed on.' Olivia wasn't absolutely sure but there was a distinct possibility that Bruce had winked at her. 'Not the first time you've been in the right place at the right time, then?'

Olivia concentrated on her soup and hoped that the hot food might provide a reason for any extra colour in her cheeks. The locals had already been talking about her. Now they would be able to embellish their stories with the knowledge that she'd stayed overnight and had just happened to be at Isaac Cameron's property when his horse had unexpectedly foaled the next morning.

That was something else about country towns, wasn't it? Everybody knew everybody else's business. She'd never want to live in a place like this. She could forgive her mother for having been appalled at the prospect. There was a lesson there, wasn't there? If you wanted a life partner, you found someone compatible and attractive who wanted the same kind of things out of life as you did and then you built a relationship that would hopefully be solid enough to last a lifetime. And, okay, she'd chosen the wrong person with Patrick but how much worse would it have been if she'd been completely in love with him? If she'd felt the kind of intense emotions that Zac was making her feel?

Ben, the paramedic, came in a few minutes later. 'Thought I could smell your soup, Betty.'

'Grab a mug, lad. There's plenty. Want a toastie?'

'Wouldn't say no.'

'You haven't been out on an ambulance call, have you?' Zac asked. 'I didn't get paged.'

'I've been cruising,' Ben told him. 'Thought I'd check in on Bert and remind him to use his spray instead of just calling us when the cold weather makes his angina worse.'

'He is one of our frequent flyers.' Zac grinned. 'Good on you for checking.'

'No worries. He lives next door to Rob, anyway, and I've put the word out that our training session for tonight is postponed until further notice.'

'I hope we can do it soon. I want to improve my abseiling techniques.'

'Abseiling?' Olivia blinked. 'I thought you were doing medical training for the local ambulance officers.'

'We swap,' Ben told her. 'Zac teaches us stuff and we teach him. Most of us are also part of the local mountain rescue team. We don't get called out that often but when we do, it can be full on.'

Debbie joined the group in the kitchen. 'Shayna and her mum got home safely. She rang to ask me to say thank you to Dr Donaldson again. She wasn't sure if she'd let her know how grateful she was that we happened to have a plastic surgeon available.'

Olivia ducked her head. 'It was a pleasure. And call me Liv. It'll save confusion if...' Her voice trailed into silence. It felt too weird to call the other Dr Donaldson her father in public.

A few looks got exchanged around the room.

'Where *is* Don?' someone asked.

Betty clicked her tongue. 'He'll be working in his office, I expect. He never looks after himself properly, that man. Someone should go and tell him to come and have some lunch.'

'I think he took his mother home,' Zac said. 'There was something she wanted to get for Liv. I imagine he'll be back very soon.'

'I heard she had a fall.' Bruce picked up another sandwich. 'I had a chat to Mike a while back and the boys had been around to board up that broken window at her place. Is she okay?'

Almost as he asked the question Mabel Donaldson appeared in the doorway of the kitchen, and Olivia wasn't the only person who was shocked by how she looked—because it was a very long way from okay. The smiling, confident woman she'd met earlier this morning was gone. Mabel looked every one of her almost ninety years right now. She also looked pale and…frightened?

'I need some help,' she said, her voice shaking. 'It's Don. He's…he's not very well…'

'Where is he?'

'In Reception.'

Zac moved first. And fast. But Olivia was right on his heels.

Jill, the receptionist, was kneeling beside the crumpled figure on the floor. She had taken off her cardigan to use as a small blanket. Zac dropped to his knees and put his hand on Don's wrist.

'What's going on?' he asked. 'What's happened?'

He looked extremely pale, Olivia noted. There were beads of sweat on his forehead and he had a bright smear of blood across his face. Zac was frowning, as if he wasn't happy with what he could feel beneath his fingers.

'Tachycardic?' she asked.

Zac nodded. 'And it's a very faint pulse. I think he's hypotensive.'

'Where's that blood come from?'

Don rubbed at his face. 'It's nothing,' he muttered. 'Just give me a hand up, will you?' He looked past Zac and Olivia and she realised that everybody else had followed them from the kitchen. They were all looking extremely anxious. Betty had her arm around Mabel.

'He had a terrible pain,' Mabel told them. 'In his stomach. He almost couldn't get out of the car. And then he was sick everywhere and...and...' She had to gulp in a deep breath. 'I've never *seen* so much blood...'

Zac caught Olivia's gaze. They both knew how serious this was. Don was showing the symptoms of hypovolaemic shock from potentially dangerous blood loss.

'Bruce? Ben?' Zac sounded calm. 'Help me carry Don into the procedures room.'

'I can walk,' Don protested. 'Stop making such a fuss.'

'Stop arguing,' Zac told him. 'This time we're in charge. Me and Liv. Okay?'

Olivia was watching her father's face so she felt the instant he made eye contact with her. He looked scared, which was under-standable because he would be well aware of the significance of vomiting blood like that. He also looked as if there was a lot he wanted to say to her and she could read a plea in his expression. Was that a plea to help him survive? Or that he would have the opportunity to say whatever it was on his mind? Or…it could have been just a plea to stay close. To let her know that he wanted her to be with him.

It didn't matter.

Olivia wasn't going anywhere.

This mattered.

Not just because any life-or-death situa-tion mattered. Or that this patient was a col-league he'd come to respect and like very much. It mattered because he'd seen the fear in Olivia's eyes. She might not be ready to forgive her father but she was most definitely not ready to lose him, either. She might be conflicted but she cared a lot more than she wanted to admit.

It was Zac who examined Don while Olivia was inserting an IV line and putting up a bag of fluids to start managing his low blood pressure. Debbie put an oxygen mask on their reluctant patient and then some ECG dots to attach him to the monitor.

'Sharp scratch,' Olivia warned when she had cleaned the skin above his vein with an alcohol wipe. 'There we go… Now, don't move while I get this cannula taped down.'

'Didn't feel a thing,' Don told her.

He could certainly feel Zac's hand on his abdomen. 'That hurts, doesn't it?'

Don couldn't hide the fact that he was in pain. 'Of course it does. It's been hurting for some time. It's only to be expected with this disease I've got.'

Debbie looked shocked. 'What disease?' she asked.

Zac gave his head a single shake. 'Nothing's been confirmed,' he told Debbie. Then he looked back at Don. 'And as far as I know, sudden onset abdominal pain along with vomiting a large amount of blood is not a symptom of pancreatic cancer. It's far more likely to be a perforated peptic ulcer.'

Don just grunted as Zac palpated another quadrant of his abdomen. 'Your blood pressure is in your boots and you're showing other signs of hypovolaemic shock. You must have lost a significant amount of blood.'

'He's still tachycardic at one twenty.' Olivia was watching the ECG trace on the monitor screen. 'And his blood pressure's dropped even further. Systolic's down to ninety. How far away is the nearest blood bank?'

'Too far,' Zac admitted. 'But we do keep a limited supply of blood products here. Some O-negative packed red cells and some plasma. They're in the second fridge in the staffroom. Debbie, could you go and get a bag of the PRC, please?' He caught Olivia's gaze as Debbie left the room and they both acknowledged the real problem they had here. They weren't going to be able to transport her father to a larger hospital any time soon and they weren't going to be able to get more blood products delivered. If this was a perforated ulcer Don could still be losing a potentially dangerous amount of blood. Right now it didn't matter that his self-diagnosis might have been completely wrong because this could still prove to be fatal and even more rapidly.

'We could do with a CT scan,' he added. 'But we'll have to make do with what we've got. An ultrasound and then an upright chest X-ray. If we see any free air under the diaphragm on X-ray then we can be a lot more sure of a perforation.'

And then what?

Surgery?

In an operating theatre that hadn't been used in a very long time?

Don gave a strangled groan and then tried

to turn onto his side. Electrodes popped off his chest and an alarm began to sound on the monitor. Olivia grabbed her father's shoulders.

'What's going on? What's wrong, Dad?'

Zac barely registered what she had called Don as they both dealt with another vomiting episode. Another several hundred mils of blood lost. But he remembered as they reassessed Don's condition to find that his level of consciousness was dropping sharply and they worked together to put a central line in so that they could deliver more fluids and the blood products that were obviously needed urgently. It was undoubtedly the first time she had called her father "Dad" since she'd been a small child. There was nothing like a crisis to make it obvious what was really important, was there? Olivia's anger at her father for her apparent abandonment was irrelevant when she was face to face with the possibility of watching him die.

Surgery was needed urgently if that wasn't going to happen.

'How are you with giving a general anaesthetic?' he asked Olivia quietly a short time later when they had stabilised Don well enough to do the tests that increased Zac's confidence in his diagnosis.

'I did a six-month rotation in anaesthetics. It was near the top of my list for a chosen speciality.' She held his gaze. 'You said you worked in war zones and on trauma teams but did that include any surgical experience?'

'I qualified as a specialist trauma surgeon before I went anywhere near a war zone. I've worked in major hospitals in the UK and the USA since then and my last position was Chief of Trauma Surgery in the biggest hospital in Chicago.' He wasn't telling her his credentials to try and impress her. He simply wanted to reassure Olivia enough for that fear in her eyes to lessen.

'We can do this,' he told her. 'As long as we do it together.'

He saw the way her chin came up and it was a familiar gesture already. A sign that she was gathering her courage and that she was prepared to face a situation she really didn't want to be in. Once again, he felt proud of her but this time there was also a wash of a much stronger feeling. Of caring. Of feeling as invested in a successful outcome here as she was because the alternative of Olivia being hurt again was unacceptable.

Sterile drapes were rolled around surgical instruments that were kept sterilised so that they could be available in an emergency but no one had ever expected that Cutler's Creek Hospital would have to deal with trying to save the life of the doctor who'd kept this hospital going almost single-handedly against the risk of closure. The son of the man who'd devoted *his* entire life to the medical needs of this community.

Don Donaldson was under general anaesthetic now and it was his daughter who was monitoring his vital signs, the blood transfusion and the medications being administered. She nodded in response to Zac's silent question. They were good to go.

Zac was scrubbed and gowned. So was

Debbie, who'd come into Theatre with them to assist.

'I'm not sure I remember what the names of some of the instruments are,' Debbie said anxiously. 'It's a long time since I did any theatre training.'

'You'll be fine,' Zac told her. 'I'll tell you which ones and what to do as we go along. The first thing I need is easy. A scalpel, please.'

There was only one goal on his mind as he made his midline incision and then started a thorough examination of the abdominal cavity, and that was to stop whatever bleeding was going on. Don Donaldson might well have to be taken back to Theatre once he reached an expert in the field at a main hospital but if whatever blood vessel had ruptured wasn't taken care of right now, he would never get that far.

Zac had to resist the urge to work too swiftly, which could mean he might miss what he was looking for. He had to coach Debbie in assisting him, to find the instruments he needed and how to manage the suction. He also had another part of his brain that needed managing and that was his awareness of Olivia at the head of the bed, watching over her father and watching *him*...

And he was too aware of her.

Their roles were reversed this time but he was strongly reminded of when he'd been the spectator, watching Olivia's skill in suturing Shayna's facial laceration. When he'd realised that somehow Olivia Donaldson had almost instantly got past any protective barriers he had in place to prevent himself caring too much about other people. Barriers that had been added to and added to until they were too big and too strong and he'd feared that he would never truly care about anything again.

'There it is.'

'A perforation?'

'Yep. The bleeding's coming from the gastroduodenal artery.' Zac adjusted the tilt of the powerful light above them, swabbed the area he had identified and watched the blood well swiftly back into the space. 'Okay… I need a suture now, Debbie. Yes…that one at the top of the tray. And a needle holder. And then I need you to help keep things visible by using the swabs and suction. How're things looking at your end, Liv?'

'Blood pressure's still on the low side. I'm going to hang that second bag of packed red cells. He's throwing off a few ectopic beats, too. The sooner you can stop that bleeding the better, Zac.'

'I'm on it.'

He was. He'd be able to stop this life-threatening blood loss within seconds. With the curved suture needles secure in the holder, Zac moved to ligate the artery before repairing the perforation by excising the ulcer that had created it.

And that's when it happened.

His hand shook.

Just for a heartbeat, and it was probably imperceptible to those watching what he was doing but it felt huge to Zac and he froze for another heartbeat because he knew why it was happening. There was too much resting on the outcome of what he was about to do. This wasn't a purely clinical challenge that needed only the best of the abilities he knew he had. Not only did he care a great deal about the man on this operating table, he was desperate to do whatever it took to protect his patient's daughter.

He cared *that* much about Olivia Donaldson.

And it felt too much like love…

Too much like the overwhelming emotion he'd felt for Mia and a reminder of the devastation and guilt that had come so close to destroying him. And, while it was a good thing that he had healed from the dead space he'd been in emotionally when he first came to Cutler's Creek, he'd only wanted to open windows in that barrier that protected his heart—this felt like a door was opening.

One that he might actually want to step through.

He didn't. He couldn't. He had to slam that door shut.

Maybe it had only affected him for a split second but that was enough. Zac used every ounce of his determination to get past that blip and focus completely on what he was doing. There would be time later to reflect on the fact that he'd faced his worst fear—that caring too much really would make it impossible to do his job to the best of his ability—and, even though he could get past it, he'd been right to fear it because maybe next time it would be worse. When it was appropriate to think about that, he would take the time and action that was needed to regain control and make sure it never happened again.

But not yet.

'Gotcha…' There was huge satisfaction to be found in lifting that swab and seeing no new blood loss. Now he could turn his focus to cleaning out the abdominal cavity as thoroughly as possible before closing up and starting Don on antibiotics. Then they would just need to monitor him and manage anything else until he could be evacuated for more definitive care, hopefully within the next few hours.

'Blood pressure's coming up already... Good job, Zac.'

He didn't look up from what he was doing. He didn't want to see respect or gratitude or anything else in Olivia's gaze. He didn't want to see those extraordinary eyes again right now or feel the connection that he knew would kick him right in the gut. The sooner this was over the better. Not just this emergency surgery but his time with Olivia.

If only he'd known...

He would never have left that voicemail on her phone.

How extraordinary...

They'd faced a challenge that could have gone very wrong even in a major hospital and they'd done with minimal staff and resources but they had succeeded against the odds.

No wonder the people who had gathered in the reception area of Cutler's Creek Community Hospital looked like they were collectively holding their breath as Olivia walked in to tell them the news.

'The surgery was successful,' she announced. 'Dr Donaldson is stable for now and we'll be able to transfer him to Dunedin as soon as the weather allows for a chopper to get here.'

'Shouldn't be too far away,' Bruce said. 'The storm's blowing through faster than expected and the wind's started dropping already. I'll get a road crew out straight away to start dealing with that slip in the gorge, too, in case we need a Plan B to go by road.' He cleared his throat and sounded as though emotions were doing their best to break through his professional focus. 'This is…this is such *great* news…'

Mabel Donaldson was wiping her eyes with a handful of tissues as she came towards Olivia.

'Oh, my dear…thank you. I was *so* worried…'

'I know. He's still not completely out of the

woods, but we've stopped the bleeding and that was the critical thing to do.'

Mabel opened the clasp of the old-fashioned handbag she was clutching. 'This is for you, Olivia.' The embossed envelope she pulled out of her bag was sealed and Olivia's name was written on the front. 'It's an invitation to my birthday party. I do hope you'll be able to come. It's far enough away for Don to be back home by then, I hope.'

'I hope so, too.' Olivia accepted the envelope but didn't clarify which of those hopes she shared. There was no way she would be heading back here for a party in the near future but her grandmother was clearly a lovely woman and she didn't deserve to be rejected in public.

'There's something else, too.' Mabel had a wallet in her hands now. 'This is Don's,' she told Olivia, as she opened it and fished inside a small pocket. 'And this is what he's carried with him for the last thirty years.'

It was a small photograph of a young girl. A photograph of Olivia taken when she'd been about four or five years old. Golden curls, big blue eyes and the happiest smile ever. Had it been her father who'd taken the photograph? The one who had been on the receiving end of that smile?

'There's so much I want to tell you,' Mabel said quietly. 'But it'll have to wait until another time. Bruce is taking me home so I can pack a bag for Don and for myself, if they'll let me go with him, and get back here before the helicopter arrives, but…could you give him his wallet, please?' She tucked the photograph back into its pocket. 'He'll want to have this with him now, I expect.'

Olivia took the wallet. She had no choice when it was being pressed into her hand like this. How could she refuse when Mabel was looking up at her so trustingly? So lovingly…

'He loves you, darling,' her grandmother said. 'And so do I. We're family, even though it might not feel like it quite yet. You'll always have a home here, you know, if you ever need a new one.'

Olivia opened her mouth to say she already had a new home and it was in the country's biggest city about as far away as you could get from a place like Cutler's Creek but the words got stuck somewhere in her throat. It might be an unwelcome connection but she had ties to this place that she would be aware of for the rest of her life. Mabel was right about her having family here.

And Zac was here, as well.

He was in the room with her father when she went in with his wallet. Debbie and Ben had wheeled a comfortable hospital bed into the procedures room and Don was lying propped up on soft pillows, surrounded by the machine monitoring his heart rhythm and blood pressure, the IV poles and lines that were still providing fluids, blood products and medication, and the oxygen tank that was attached to the mask he was wearing. He looked drowsy but his eyelids flickered open as Oliva entered the room and she knew he was watching her.

Zac was also watching her and he held her

gaze for a heartbeat before his lips curved into a smile. A tiny moment of time that was enough for Olivia to realise how fierce the connection between the two of them had become in such a very short time.

'Everything's stable,' he told her. 'But could you stay with your dad for a few minutes, please? I need to write up as detailed a report of the surgery as I can for the team he's going to be transferred to.'

'Sure.'

'I'll be in my office if you need me. That's next door to your dad's office, if you remember where that is?'

Olivia gave a single nod. She hadn't forgotten where she'd had that horribly awkward meeting with her father for the first time in decades. Her hand tightened around the shape of the wallet she was holding. So many years and he'd been carrying a photograph of her in his wallet for that entire time?

'I'll be in Theatre for a bit,' Debbie said. 'I need to start cleaning up in there.' She tilted her head at Ben as if encouraging him to leave the room, as well.

'I'd better make sure the ambulance is ready,' he said hurriedly. 'Just in case we need to meet land transport for Dr Donaldson halfway or something—if a chopper can't get here.'

If they'd agreed on a plan to try and leave Olivia alone with her father, it had worked remarkably well.

'Your…um… Mabel gave me this to give to you.' She put the wallet on the table beside the bed. 'She's gone to get a bag packed for you to take to hospital but she thought you might want to keep this with you.'

Don reached for the wallet. The movement was clearly painful and he couldn't reach. Olivia picked the wallet up and put it close enough to his hand for him to take it but Don's hand closed around hers instead. With his other hand, he pulled the oxygen mask away from his face.

'Thank you,' he said softly. 'Zac said he couldn't have done this without you.'

'Oh, I don't know about that.' Olivia was trying to keep her tone light as she extracted her hand. It was too much to cope with right now, knowing that that photograph was caught up in the middle of that physical contact. An image of herself, before she'd been betrayed by the man she'd loved so much. 'But we did make a good team.'

'I'm very lucky you were here, though. Not just because you saved my life.'

Olivia had to look away from what she could see in her father's eyes. A gleam of something that looked like real joy. She had to clear her throat to get rid of the lump.

'This should never have happened, you know,' she told her father. 'Peptic ulcer disease is very easy to manage these days.'

'I know.' Don held the mask up to his face again and closed his eyes as he took a couple of deep breaths. 'I was stupid. Not for the first time.'

'And it didn't look like there was anything at all wrong with your pancreas when Zac did that ultrasound examination. By the time you've had a good check-up in hospital, I think you'll find you're not going to die anytime soon.'

Her voice wobbled at that point. She didn't want to lose her father. To her dismay, a single tear escaped and rolled down the side of her nose just as Don opened his eyes again.

'Oh, *Libby*…'

It wasn't just the use of that old nickname, it was the wealth of love in his tone. Olivia wasn't sure who reached out first, but the end result was that her father had his arms wrapped around her and she was back in an embrace she hadn't felt since she was a child. And it felt…as if it could be as comforting as it had always been if she could just allow herself to trust it. And it felt as if it was really going to be possible to trust it and that just made her tears fall so fast she had to extract herself and pull a handful of tissues from the box on the bedside table.

'So…' she said into the silence that followed. 'There you go. I'm glad you're not about to die.'

Don's smile was fleeting. 'I was sorry to hear about Janice's death,' he said slowly. 'It must have been hard on you, losing your mum.'

'Yeah...it's never easy losing a parent. Even if you're not that close...'

It was possible that Don would interpret that statement as applying to himself but it didn't. Looking back on her relationship with her mother, Olivia realised how distant they'd really been. That it had been a complicated dance of trying to win approval and affection. Her mother had never glowed with the kind of unconditional welcome that her newly found grandmother had displayed in the first minutes of meeting Olivia. Or spoken her name with the kind of love her father had when he'd called her "Libby" again.

'It was a tragedy that she died so young. I hope... I hope that she was happy in her life in London, though...'

'She was successful. A big name in a big city,' Olivia told him. 'And that made her happy, I think.'

Don simply nodded. He wasn't about to criticise her mother, Olivia realised. Or say anything that might be unwelcome. Maybe this was actually an unspoken agreement between them to try and leave the past in the past and move on and, for a beat, Olivia could feel sorry for her mother, in fact. How sad was it that she wouldn't have even recognised the rewards that could come from being part of a community like this because they were so different from the status and success that came from being the top of your field in a huge city? Had she really been happy with her life?

Was Olivia in danger of making the same kind of mistakes?

'I wanted to contact you when I heard she'd died,' Don added. 'I picked up the phone. I started writing you another letter but… I wasn't sure you would want to hear from me. I thought that it might be far too late. That you hated me…'

'I don't hate you,' Olivia whispered.

Not any more. She had at one point, though,

when that bewildered and sad child had grown into an angry teenager. It had been a relief to leave those teenage years and the anger behind and find a much emptier space that could keep her safe if she stayed within its boundaries. Hate and love were both intense emotions and they were more closely related than people realised. It was safer to stay in that safe space away from anything too intense and Olivia had managed to do exactly that, until she'd driven into this small town.

'And it was about then that I noticed the first symptoms of the cancer I was sure I had.' Don's breath came out in a soft groan.

'Are you in pain?'

'A bit.'

'On a scale of one to ten?'

'About a seven. Maybe eight.'

'I'll top up your analgesia.' It was a relief to have something medical to do for a few minutes. To check her patient and make sure it was safe to give him a higher dose of pain medication. To spend a minute making sure that she recorded everything on the paperwork that would go with him to the hospital.

The extra medication was enough to let Don sink back against his pillows with a sigh of relief. He closed his eyes.

'They're still there,' he said, his words a little slurred. 'The letters. In that box. Take them with you, if you want.'

Don appeared to have fallen asleep as he finished speaking because he didn't stir when Olivia gently pulled his oxygen mask back into place. Her fingers touched his cheek as she did so and she found she had to swallow past another huge lump in her throat.

She had never stopped loving her father—she had just buried those feelings long enough to make them disappear. Was it really possible to tap back into the love that had been there in her earliest years? To make up for all those years that had been lost, even? An almost desperate longing was being balanced by fear, however. She would have to step out of her safe space and that would be taking a huge risk.

Was she brave enough to do that? If she went and got that box of letters, would she be brave enough to read them?

'Liv?' Her gaze flicked up to find Zac was standing in the door. 'The chopper's on its way. It'll be here in thirty minutes. Can I borrow you for a bit? Debbie's coming in to watch Don and I need your notes on his anaesthetic for the transfer report.'

'Of course.' But Olivia let her gaze rest on him for another beat before she moved.

Zac was still wearing the scrubs that he'd had on under his Theatre gown. He still had a line across his forehead where the elastic of his cap had been a little too tight and he must have fluffed up his hair to have it as rumpled as it was again now. He wasn't smiling but there was a warmth in those gorgeous caramel-brown eyes that Olivia could feel right into her bones and it came with a tingle of the kind of excitement and joy she hadn't felt since she'd been very young.

She had assumed that not feeling things this intensely was simply a part of growing up and becoming a sensible adult and it was a complete revelation that it could still happen. But it was also as scary and wonderful and confusing as the beginnings of reconnecting with her father. The only thing Olivia could be absolutely sure of in this moment was just how far she had already stepped out of any safe place.

There was no going back.

CHAPTER EIGHT

'PROBLEM?'

'No, not at all.' Olivia eased herself into the seat behind the desk in Zac's office. She had no problem with complying with the request to add to the report he was making on her father's surgery. She'd just been a little disconcerted to sink into a seat that felt like it was still holding the warmth of Zac's body because it was doing odd things to her own body, like making her heart speed up and her breath feel like it was catching as that warmth in her belly became that distinctive tingle of desire.

'I'll just need five minutes,' she added, taking a folded piece of paper from her pocket. 'I've got my record of all the drugs I used during the anaesthetic and my monitoring of his vital signs.'

'I'll come back in a few minutes, then. Hit "print" when you're finished. I'll just check that Debbie's still okay monitoring Don and that Bruce knows to clear any debris from the car park before the helicopter comes in to land. There must be quite a lot of broken branches after the winds we've had today. You planning to fly with him?'

'No.' Olivia shook her head. 'I'll keep in touch with his progress, of course, but Mabel will be going with him. I was only supposed to be away for a day so I'm already very late getting back to Auckland and it's not as though I can just abandon my rental car here in the back of beyond.'

There was something odd in Zac's expression but he turned away too quickly for Olivia to try and interpret it.

'Of course not,' was all he said as he left the office.

Writing a succinct medical report was easy enough to be almost automatic. The focus required still allowed for a part of Olivia's brain to be trying to process other things.

Like the confusion she'd been grappling with as she'd followed Zac to his office to do this task. That tumble of emotions that was undermining her ability to think straight. Joy. Fear. Excitement. Relief. Trust. They all felt too new and fragile. Bubbles of sensation that might pop if she tried to catch them to see if they were real. And that confusion that had just ramped up a little in the aftermath of that look on Zac's face when she'd said she was already too late in getting back to Auckland.

There was an echo of Mabel's voice in there somewhere, too.

'You'll always have a home here, you know, if you ever need a new one.'

But Cutler's Creek was the last place she belonged in. Wasn't it?

She hadn't wanted to be here this long. So why did she feel as if she wasn't ready to leave yet? Why did she feel as if all she wanted to do right now was go over to where that leather jacket was hanging on a hook on the back of the door? To put her cheek against the lining of that jacket perhaps and inhale deeply to find out whether there was any lingering scent of the man who'd been wearing it?

She had her chance to do that when she went over to the printer to see why the report hadn't emerged, despite the sound of the machine working. A red light was flashing on the control panel and it appeared that the printer had run out of paper. Olivia was looking around to see where a new ream might be stored when the door opened right beside her and Zac stepped in so swiftly he almost collided with her.

'Oh…sorry. I didn't see you.'

'No worries… I'm…ah…looking for some more paper for the printer.'

'It's there.' Zac pushed the door shut behind him, nodding towards a shelf that had been partially hidden by the door. 'I can do that.'

But they both moved at the same time, ending up even closer to each other, and, for the longest moment, it felt like time stood still. Olivia's mouth went dry as she held her breath, remembering how they'd both moved together at the same time yesterday evening and ended up this close to each other. She was reliving that thrill of sensation she'd had when Zac had taken her wine glass out of her hand and that look in his eyes had told her exactly what was going to happen in the next few seconds. She just hadn't known that that kiss would be the first move of a kind of lovemaking so amazing she would never have believed she would ever experience it.

The pull towards this man was so astonishingly powerful it was scrambling her brain completely. Like giving in to a human magnet, Olivia just wanted to press herself against his body. To lift her face and look into his eyes so that he knew just how much she wanted to kiss him. No…make that throw her arms around his neck and pull his head down so that she didn't have to wait a second longer to feel his lips touching hers. To feel that heat and a taste that she would never, ever be able to get enough of…

But Zac made a strangled sound that could have been interpreted as irritation and Olivia froze as he moved around her to pick up the ream of paper and tear the wrapping open.

'Bruce tells me that they've got one lane open in the gorge now.' His voice sounded slightly hoarse, which was probably why Zac cleared his throat. 'It'll be a slow trip but you should be able to make it back to Dunedin today. Unless…'

Olivia's heart skipped a beat. What was he going to suggest? That she might want to stay a bit longer?

He wasn't looking at her as he opened a drawer of the printer and slotted the new supply of paper into place. 'Unless you want to do something to really help your dad recuperate,' he added.

'How do you mean?'

'We'll probably need a locum if it's going to take a while until he's back on his feet properly.' Zac still wasn't turning to meet her gaze. 'I thought maybe you'd like a chance to get to know your gran. Stay for her birthday party, maybe. You left your invitation in the procedures room, by the way.'

It felt like he was asking more than whether she would like a chance to get to know her grandmother. Was he offering Olivia the opportunity to get to know *him* better? Was Zac feeling something like the overwhelming connection to her that she had found with him? Was he afraid that the person he might have been destined to share his life with was about to walk out, never to be seen again?

'I…*can't*…' The words came out as a whisper. It felt as if they were being dragged out because something was fighting that conviction.

You don't really want to leave, a tiny voice was insisting in her head. Or was it her heart? *You might think this is the back of beyond, and that you'd never want to live in a rural town, but that's not true, is it? That sense of space that the mountains and land give you here doesn't really make you feel intimidated, does it? It makes you feel free. You don't need a crumpled photograph to convince you that your father has never really stopped loving you. Part of you has always wanted to believe that—you were just too scared to take the risk of finding out you might be wrong. And what about Zac? You don't still believe there's no such thing as love at first sight, do you?*

Talk about having your head messed with. This was too powerful. It couldn't be trusted. Or…maybe that was exactly what she needed to do.

Trust it.

She should have trusted her father more. Maybe she could trust Zac as well?

She wanted him to step closer. To take her into his arms and tell her that Auckland was not the right place for her. To persuade her to stay here, at least long enough to find out for sure whether there was something real about this fantasy she'd stepped into with Zac.

But he turned to collect the printed pages that were appearing in the tray so she opened her mouth to speak herself. To say that she'd need a couple of days to sort things out in

Auckland but that she would come back just as soon as she could—if he wanted her to.

It was Zac who spoke first, however.

'Don't let what happened last night put you off,' he said. 'I can promise it wouldn't happen again.'

Olivia froze. Why not? Could he dismiss last night *that* easily? Did he not even have the slightest desire for it to happen again?

'Besides,' Zac added, 'I won't be here much longer myself.'

He'd hurt her by being so dismissive.

Maybe it had been inevitable that she was going to be hurt but there was no relief to be found in the sudden distance Zac could feel between them. The way Olivia had been looking at him when he'd come into this office had made him doubt his ability to control what was going on in his head. He still wanted to drop this sheaf of papers he had in his hands and grab Olivia's shoulders. To close the physical distance between them and dip his head—to breathe in the scent of her hair and skin. To kiss her and then kiss her again and never bother coming up for air. To take her home and shut the door and make everything and everyone else in the world irrelevant for as long as possible.

The desire to do exactly that was just as bad as that momentary wobble he'd experienced in Theatre today. Or the way he'd acted so instinctively to protect Olivia when that plane wreckage had exploded. They were all signs that he was starting to feel things too much again. It wasn't simply that he was risking opening the doors to flashbacks that could be terrifying in their intensity. He wanted to keep Olivia close. To say something that would persuade her to stay in Cutler's Creek. The way he had persuaded Mia to stay for those extra few weeks? The extra weeks that had taken her life? He couldn't live with that kind of guilt again. He knew what he had to do but, dear Lord, it was hard.

'You've reminded me that there's a lot more to life than an isolated place like this,' he carried on. 'I only ever came here on a temporary basis and I'm ready to get back to the real world. It's time to move on. Another war zone, perhaps. They're always short of volunteers and things don't get any more real than that.'

He was thinking out loud, really, so it didn't matter if no one else heard him but the silence coming from Olivia was so profound that Zac had to look up to make sure that she hadn't somehow slipped out the office while he'd been collecting the printout of that report.

And then he wished he hadn't looked up.

Those eyes…

For a horrible instant, Zac had a glimpse of what he could imagine Olivia had looked like as a child. When she'd believed that her father had walked out on her life without a backward glance. She looked lost. Bewildered. As vulnerable as it was possible for anyone to look. She'd look like that if she was being dumped. How crazy was it to feel like that was exactly what he *was* doing? But it had to be done. And done convincingly enough to make sure it was really done, for both their sakes. Giving in to the disturbingly intense emotional reaction he was having to this woman might only end up hurting her more. What if she stayed here because of him and she became unhappy? Or, worse, that something terrible happened to her? He couldn't do it. It was too big. And it was too destructive when it went wrong.

The best way to be convincing was to be honest, wasn't it?

'I'm sorry,' he said quietly. 'But it's who I am now. I can't get attached. To places. Or people.'

'You can't just walk away from your responsibilities here.' Her voice was tight. 'You'd leave Cutler's Creek without a doctor. The hospital will get closed down.'

'I'll advertise for a locum, unless you want to change your mind about staying?'

She avoided his glance. 'And you'll stay until you find one?'

'If I can. Your dad managed pretty well by

himself for a long time before I came here. It takes a special kind of person to want to live in a place like this, I guess. Maybe this time we can try and find a couple of married doctors who like the idea of running their own hospital and bringing their kids up in a pretty magical part of the world. That way, Don could retire any time he wants to.'

'You can't do that. He might think that he's not wanted any more. This is *his* hospital.'

Zac almost smiled. 'You sound like you care,' he said quietly. He was reminded again for a moment about the assumptions he'd made about Olivia when he'd left that voicemail—that she was someone who could simply walk away from someone that loved her. That she had no compassion for others.

How wrong had he been? She'd been in there, boots and all, to help save that pilot's life. She'd helped deliver Chloe's foal and had missed her chance to get away from Cutler's Creek because she'd taken the time to retrace her steps to tell him about the birth so he could make sure the foal was kept safe.

And she'd been so afraid that she might lose her father today. How ironic was that when the only reason she'd come here in the first place had been because she had believed he was about to die and wanted to tell him how little she thought of him? From the atmosphere he'd felt in the room between father and daughter when he'd gone in to find Olivia, something huge had changed for the better.

Life could change in an instant, couldn't it?

Things you had come to believe were absolute truths could be thrown into doubt. Like being able to fall in love again? It was confusing. Alarming.

Olivia was staring at him. 'Why wouldn't I care? My grandfather worked here. I expect my father will work here again as soon as he's back on his feet because I don't think he's anywhere near ready to retire. His mother's about to have a significant birthday and knowing that the hospital might be closed would not be a great way to celebrate that occasion, would it?'

'And you think that's *my* responsibility? It's your family, Olivia.'

'You can't tell me you don't care. Well, you can and you did and maybe you even believe it yourself but I saw how hard it was for you to operate on someone you care about but you did it, Zac. You saved my dad's life. And I don't believe that you're going to let him lose what matters most to him.'

Oh, God…she'd seen that momentary hesitation in Theatre. Of course she had. She'd seen the flashback he'd had when that plane had exploded and she'd known exactly how significant that had been. Had she also known why that tiny wobble had happened? That it hadn't just been the respect he had for her father that had made it matter so much but how he was feeling about Olivia herself? He couldn't say anything. Because…

Because he didn't dare admit—to himself, let alone someone else—that he cared that much.

Because caring that much was something he simply couldn't allow himself to do again.

He knew where that led to. That dark space. Where it was too real and too raw to pretend it was any kind of a movie. He'd learned how to control his mind. And his heart—in the same way he'd finally gained control of those flashbacks after Mia had died. Sure, he'd come here to try and balance that control because not feeling anything was just as bad as feeling too much, but the seesaw was teetering too much right now. The holes in that protective wall were getting too big. If he didn't take control he might lose himself and that couldn't be allowed to happen. It was very obvious what the first step in taking that control back needed to be. To get far enough away from this woman who was messing with his head. And his life.

'I already told you what matters most to your dad,' he said as he stepped past Olivia to get to the door. 'But that wasn't enough to make you want to stay, was it?'

Nothing could have made Olivia stay a minute longer than she absolutely had to so she was in that rental car heading back to the airport in Dunedin almost as soon as the helicopter evacuating her father had disappeared in the same direction.

She'd said goodbye. She'd told her father and grandmother that she would be calling the hospital regularly to get updated on his progress and that she would be in touch as soon as she'd had time to get her head around everything.

She was still wearing hospital scrubs under her coat because that had been preferable to putting Zac's borrowed clothes back on. If she didn't find something new at the airport, she'd just fly back to Auckland like this because she was that desperate to try and find the solid foundations of the life she had chosen for herself again. She'd told Zac that she'd post the scrubs back as soon as she'd had them laundered.

'Don't bother,' he'd said. *'They're no great loss.'*

He wasn't bothered that she was leaving, either. He'd just told her to drive carefully and then raised a hand in farewell as he'd walked back inside the hospital without a backward glance.

It was still raining but the damaging winds had lessened and she'd been assured that the road was passable as long as she took enough care.

'Not that we're chasing you out of town or anything,' Bruce said after updating her on road conditions in the gorge. 'And we're all hoping you'll be back real soon now that you and your dad have reconnected. When the doc gets out of hospital, maybe?'

'Yes, of course. But I'm not sure how soon that will be.'

All she wanted was to get going and put as many miles as possible between herself and Cutler's Creek.

Between herself and Isaac Cameron.

There was no pause to swipe away tears near the rugby field this time. It was tempting for a moment to stop at Zac's house and go and have a peep at Chloe and her foal but Olivia knew she couldn't afford the time and it would only make it more difficult to settle the confused emotions that kept ambushing her. At least there was no chance of a plane crashing to bring her journey to an unexpected halt this time and no irresistibly attractive doctor with an Irish accent to ply her with wine and make her break so many of her own rules.

Well, she'd learned her lesson, that was for sure.

Olivia might not have been crying as she drove away from both old and new memories but she'd never felt so...hollow.

Empty.

Crushed, even.

And how stupid was that? She barely knew Zac. It shouldn't matter that he had so little interest in her that he couldn't wait to get out of the country and head back into some war zone. It really, really shouldn't make her feel like she'd been dumped, let alone that she'd been abandoned. That she had been prepared to take the risk to trust someone and that trust had been broken—again. It was casting a shadow on the hope that she and her father could rebuild their relationship. Feeding into a fear that Olivia had always had— that, deep down, maybe there was something wrong with her that made men not want to stay around…

Oh, let it go, Olivia told herself sternly. *You knew all along that over-the-top emotional reactions can never be trusted. That disappointment was the best outcome you could hope for and that devastation was the real risk.* Her mother had taught her, by example, that staying in control and true to your ambitions was the key to success in life and you could only stay in control if you didn't give in to emotions that probably wouldn't last very long anyway.

Was that why she'd been sent to boarding school at such a young age?

Why her mother might have felt quite justified in changing her mind about going to work in a country hospital with the man she must have loved enough to marry?

Why she might have tried to teach her

daughter that a career was more important than relationships with people?

Was Olivia like her mother because she had inherited her personality traits or was it due to the way she'd been brought up? No. She *wasn't* like her mother. Not at all. If she ever had a child, she'd make sure it knew it was loved. She wouldn't send it away to boarding schools and she would call it "darling" at every possible opportunity. She knew that from now on her father was going to be a part of her life—she just didn't know how big a part that would be.

That small box of letters and parcels was on the back seat of this car. But there were still echoes of her mother's voice there, too. Warning her not to throw away the belief that her career was the most important thing in her life. It was too hard to keep a coherent thread of thought going so Olivia knew she had to give up and just let things settle in her head.

She wasn't going to think about it any more right now. She could see the flashing lights ahead that were a warning of the road crew that were clearing the slide of mud and rocks on the narrow gorge road. She needed to focus completely on her driving from now on and make sure she reached the airport safely.

Hopefully, there would be a late plane she could take to Auckland. A shop that was open for some form of clothing. And a phone charger. She needed to ring the hospital and find out how her father was doing because, once she knew that he was going to be fine, she could draw a line under this extraordinary couple of days and normal life could resume.

Nothing felt normal.

When the rain had stopped a few hours after Don had been evacuated Zac had made a late round to check on the few inpatients at Cutler's Creek Community Hospital. He had phoned Shayna's mother to remind her that extra pillows were needed for tonight to help any facial swelling to go down and he'd spoken to Faye Morris to check that all was well now that she was at home, coping with her toddler as well as her newborn baby.

Now *he* was at home, too, and there was a newborn baby in the barn. The foal had astonishingly long, gangly legs that were already fluffy, and Chloe rubbed her head up and down Zac's arm as if nodding in response to being told how clever she was to produce such a beautiful baby. It was warm and cosy in the barn and there was a lovely smell that was a mixture of sweet straw and hay and horse but eventually Zac had to go inside the house and he knew the minute he walked in that he'd had good reason to be dreading this moment.

There were dishes piled up in the sink. There was the frying pan he'd used to cook the eggs in the middle of last night and plates that were still smeared with the onion jam they'd put into those sandwiches. The room felt so empty that Zac had the weird impression that he was catching a glimpse of Olivia from the corner of his eye. A ghostlike image that was felt rather than seen and it made his skin prickle. It was going to be worse in the bedroom. Even if those rumpled sheets didn't still hold an echo of her scent, he wouldn't be able to lie there without re-living every single moment of the most astonishing night of his life.

Well…he could fix that. He just needed something else to think about, didn't he? Dealing with the dishes in the sink was a good start. He'd change the sheets on his bed as well, but not just yet. Taking his laptop from his bag, Zac sat down and logged onto a website he had used many times before.

There would be more than one place in the world where Doctors without Borders would be currently more than welcome. Like Afghanistan and Yemen. Bangladesh, Bolivia and Myanmar. Sadly, there were more than seventy countries in the world that were in need of the humanitarian assistance Zac was more than qualified to provide.

He just needed to decide where in the world he wanted to go next.

CHAPTER NINE

THE OVAL WINDOW of the plane framed a very familiar cityscape with the needle point of the Sky Tower amongst high-rise buildings and the gorgeous backdrop of the rising sun on a sparkling blue sea and scattered islands. Olivia let out her breath in a heartfelt sigh as the plane banked to head away from the central city towards the airport.

'Gorgeous, isn't it?' The man in the seat next to her was leaning to see out of the window, as well. 'It's no wonder that Auckland gets rated every year as one of the top cities in the world for quality of life. I certainly wouldn't want to live anywhere else.'

'Me neither,' Olivia murmured, stamping on any tiny voice in the back of her head that might try arguing with that.

'Been away on holiday?'

'Not exactly.' She offered a wry smile to her fellow passenger on this red-eye flight from Dunedin. 'It was supposed to be a day trip but I got caught out by a storm in Central Otago.'

'Oh… I think I saw something about that on TV. Or was it a plane crash or something?'

Olivia made a noncommittal sound and was grateful for the announcement about putting away tray tables and making sure her seat was in the upright position for landing. She wasn't about to start telling a stranger about her unexpected adventures. She could feel her lips curling into another almost-smile as she imagined the questions that would have come her way if she had still been wearing the scrubs she had borrowed from Cutler's Creek Hospital.

It had been a blessing in disguise that there'd been no late-evening flights from Dunedin last night. The five-star hotel she had chosen had not only offered a luxurious room and range of beauty products but there was also a boutique clothing shop that they were only too happy to open for her to choose a new outfit—the kind of skirt and jacket that was entirely appropriate for her position as a private surgeon.

The two-hour direct flight had left Dunedin before dawn and she was going straight to the Plastic Surgery Institute. She would hopefully be able to step seamlessly back into her work and her real life would fold itself around her. Surely she only needed to be back where she belonged to know that everything was going to be okay? She agreed wholeheartedly with her neighbour's sentiments about this city and she could feel her spirits lifting noticeably as the plane's wheels bumped onto the tarmac. She wouldn't want to live anywhere else in the world. This was where she had been born. This was home.

More than an hour later, Olivia was still in the back of a taxi, caught up in a traffic jam on Auckland's motorway system because there had been an accident somewhere miles ahead of her. Sitting there in four lanes of bumper-to-bumper traffic was bad enough but then it started to rain. Watching the drops splatter onto the windows and then trickle down the glass made it impossible not to get dragged back into memories from the last couple of days.

Like the splatter of rain on a tin roof that had made being in Isaac Cameron's bed even more cosy.

Feeling the rain on her skin as she'd carried that huge foal into the barn.

And...*oh*... Zac's touch on her skin...

The ringtone of her phone was a jerk back to reality and Olivia snatched it from her bag. Part of her brain was still letting go of what had just been on her mind with such startling clarity, however, so she actually thought it might be Zac calling her and her heart rate accelerated as she looked at the screen, expecting the call to be from an unknown number. It wasn't. It was her boss.

'Simon... I'm so sorry. I thought I'd be at the Institute a lot sooner than this.' Would Simon notice that her tone was artificially bright? 'That bad weather seems to have followed me up the country and I'm stuck on the motorway now.'

'Not to worry. Your first appointment's not till eleven. I'm sure you'll get here by then.'

'I certainly hope so. I can't believe how bad this traffic is.' Olivia looked out of the window as she spoke. How different was this from driving on a country road with a backdrop of a mountain range? The closest thing she'd seen to a traffic jam around Cutler's Creek had been that mob of sheep that had escaped when they had been rescuing the pilot of that small plane.

'The downside of living in the biggest city of a small country.' Simon didn't sound upset that she was late yet again. 'Let's catch up tomorrow. I'm tied up with an out-of-town consultation for the rest of today. I can't say much yet but you'll hear all about it soon.' Simon was sounding very pleased. 'It's celebrity stuff. International... Could be the start of something big. New Zealand is the perfect place to come and hide away from the media if you want to get some work done and then recuperate in privacy.'

She should be interested, Olivia thought. As excited as Simon even, but she wasn't. 'Are you near your computer?' she asked. 'Could you tell me if my eleven o'clock is a new patient or someone I know?'

She needed to get her head into the right space to be ready for what the rest of this day was going to bring because Olivia had the horrible feeling that it was not going to be as easy as she'd hoped. On a par with actually getting into work, judging by how slowly this taxi was inching forward in the traffic jam.

'Someone you know,' Simon said a moment later. She could hear the smile in his voice. 'Someone we all know rather well. How 'bout that? Peggy Eglington has asked for you specifically.'

Peggy was famous for her charity work in Auckland. She was also famous for the amount of plastic surgery she'd had over the years. Had it only been a few days ago that

Olivia had reminded herself that she needed to do some more research into body dysmorphic disorder? Peggy was a prime example of the condition. She was probably due to have more filler injected into any tiny lines she was noticing. Or that she had a new bump on her nose and she couldn't believe that she had only just spotted it.

But no…arriving just in time for her first appointment, Olivia discovered that it was something else that was distressing Peggy.

'Can't you see it? I can't bear to look in a mirror. I haven't let anyone photograph me since I noticed.'

'I think you look wonderful, Peggy. You always do.'

'But…*look*…my eyes are completely different sizes. Even my eyebrows aren't even. It's that brow lift I had years ago, isn't it? Before I started coming here. Oh… I knew that was a mistake. I should make a complaint. Sue them, perhaps?'

'It was a long time ago. Things do change over time.' Olivia was having to work hard to sound sympathetic. Her patient was well into her seventies. Surely she would have to accept ageing a little more gracefully soon? Her grandmother had it nailed, she thought. About to celebrate being ninety and what you noticed about her was that the deepest creases on her face were the ones that accompanied that warm and welcoming smile.

Peggy put down the hand mirror she had been peering into so that she could show Olivia exactly what she was worried about.

'You can fix it, though, can't you? Redo the brow lift? Would that work?'

'It would be another general anaesthetic for you, Peggy. We do need to consider your problems with your blood pressure and your heart when thinking about a more major procedure like that. I wouldn't recommend it.'

'But would it work? Without leaving a visible scar?'

The mention of a scar made Olivia instantly wonder how Shayna was today and whether she had followed all the instructions to help her injury heal swiftly. She'd love to be there when the stitches came out to see whether she was justified in feeling as satisfied as she did with that work. Right now, however, she had to think about creating scars that were totally unnecessary rather than helping someone get past what could have been a disfiguring accident.

'The scars for a brow lift are hidden by the hair,' she told Peggy. 'It could certainly address the unevenness you're aware of but, as I said, there are risks—'

'No.' Peggy's head shake was firm. 'No "buts". You're not going to talk me out of it, Dr Donaldson. Book me in, please. As soon as possible.' She stood up. 'I know you're going to insist that I have all sorts of tests first but I like that about you. You're careful and that's how I know I'm in safe hands. Just call me, dear, when you've got a date for me.'

Olivia did pick up the phone later that afternoon but it wasn't to call Peggy Eglington with an admission date to the Plastic Surgery Institute's ward in the private hospital.

It was a call to a hospital at the other end of the country.

'His name's Don Donaldson,' she told the operator. 'He was brought in by helicopter yesterday afternoon from Central Otago. I imagine he's in Intensive Care?'

'Who's calling, please?'

'I'm his daughter. Olivia Donaldson.'

It didn't feel weird to say that now. It felt important. A ticket to being given some information that she was anxious to have and it was very reassuring to have her call passed to one of the doctors in the ICU.

'He's doing very well,' she was told. 'He went for endoscopy first thing this morning to see if any further surgery was needed but…' There was an incredulous huff of sound on the other end of the line as if this doctor was shaking her head. 'I can't believe that somebody could operate in a country hospital that hasn't been used for surgery for years and do such a good job. That doctor your father works with is a bit of a hero, I'd say. Cutler's Creek is lucky to have him.'

Olivia could feel a lump forming in her throat as she thought back to watching Zac performing that surgery. She felt so…proud of him? Cutler's Creek wasn't going to have him for much longer, though. She wondered if her father knew about that yet.

'If it's all good, how come he still needs to be in Intensive Care?'

'It's just a precaution. He lost a lot of blood so we'll keep a close eye on him for at least the rest of today. Oh…he's just had an MRI as well and you'll be happy to know that there's nothing obviously wrong with his pancreas at all. I think we've been able to reassure him completely that he's not about to follow in *his* father's footsteps.'

A corner of Olivia's mouth curved up. Zac would no doubt be delighted to know he'd been right about that. She could just imagine the gleam in those gorgeous brown eyes. How good would it have been to be the one to tell him that news? And that the specialists from a major centre had been so impressed with his skills in operating. Olivia could imagine exactly what it would be like to be holding that gaze. She was never going to forget doing exactly that when he'd taken that wine glass out of her hand. When they'd both known what was about to happen. Oh, *help...*

The wrench back to reality came like a physical slap.

Zac hadn't felt like that. He'd had no lingering desire to spend more time with her. He'd rather leave the country and find an exciting war zone to be in and the last image she would ever have of him was the way he had been walking away from her with one hand in the air. Without looking back.

It was weird how you could have thoughts and such powerful emotions that could overpower your mind and your soul in the space of just a heartbeat or two. Olivia tuned back into what the person on the other end of the line was telling her, having only missed a few words.

'...so we've started him on the standard triple treatment antibiotics for peptic ulcer disease, which was confirmed with the biopsy taken during the endoscopy. And he'll need to take proton pump inhibiters to reduce stomach acid but I would expect that he'll go to a ward by tomorrow morning and we're talking about transferring him back to Cutler's Creek hospital for a recuperation period by the end of the week. Now…would you like to talk to him? Or your grandmother, perhaps? I can give them this phone. Your grandmother's been telling me that you were the one to do the anaesthetic for Don. She's very proud of you.'

'Oh…?' That lump was back again at the thought of someone being genuinely proud of her. Someone who had called her "darling" as if it was the most natural thing in the world to do. 'I can't at the moment because I've got a patient waiting but I'll call again as soon as I can.'

'That's not a small cliff.'

'Don't worry, Zac. We're not about to let you fall.' Ben was grinning. 'Let's have a look at that Prusik knot you've tied and see if you remembered how to do it.'

'Bit easier doing it at home in front of the fire than out here with half-frozen fingers.'

'Looks good, though.' It was Mike, the fireman, who checked Zac's knot-tying. 'Okay…put a loop of your rope through the belay plate and then into the carabiner and screw it shut.'

Zac followed instructions and soon had both the rope and the Prusik loop attached to his harness.

'Check to make sure the loop grabs the rope if you let go. And remember to always keep your hand on the rope in front of the loop. Okay…you're good to go. Climb over the edge but don't weight the rope until you're holding onto it.'

Zac had done this before but not on a cliff anywhere near as rugged or high as this one. He was determined to learn to abseil well, though. He didn't want to have to wait until others could bring an injured climber up to him on a rescue mission. He wanted to get down the cliff and start treating them so that by the time they got the stretcher to the top, they wouldn't be wasting any more time in evacuating someone.

Not that it should still be a priority, mind you. It was several days since Zac had made the decision to move on from Cutler's Creek and it was unlikely that he would find himself a mountain rescue team to join in whatever part of the planet he landed in next.

It was also several days since Olivia Donaldson had gone back to her real life so he shouldn't even be thinking about her any more. Thinking that maybe she'd be into something as physical as this mountain rescue or abseiling, judging by the way she'd clambered around that crashed plane, determined to do whatever it took to save that pilot. Who wouldn't have been impressed by that?

'Adjust your harness if you need to,' Ben said. 'You want to make sure it's comfortable before you start the descent.'

Being about to trust his life to some ropes

and belay devices should have been enough to focus Zac's thoughts completely on what he was doing at this moment but, somehow, moving his legs to feel how the straps of his harness were gripping the top of his thighs sent his mind fleetingly in another direction that also involved Olivia, and he gave his head a slight shake to get rid of the unwanted distraction. That it was so annoying to have intrusive thoughts like this was a reminder of just how much a couple of days with Olivia had unsettled him, and the amount of effort it was taking to gain control back.

'I'm good to go.' He had his feet wide apart and was leaning back into the harness. Getting safely down this cliff was only the first part of this training exercise. There were other members of the team who were already at the bottom, along with a stretcher and a mannequin that represented the injured climber they were going to have to get back up the cliff and then carry down to their transport vehicle, which was a good hike away.

By the time the group of men were on the track leading back to where they'd parked, they were all a little weary and ready to enjoy the aftermath of a very physical session.

'So who's coming to the pub for a beer after this, then?'

'I'll come to the pub,' Zac said. 'But it's no beer for me at the moment, being the only doctor in these parts.'

'When's Don getting home?' Bruce was in front of Zac.

'Tomorrow. He's done really well.'

'He's lucky to be alive,' Ben said. 'Wouldn't be if you hadn't been there.'

'It wasn't just me.' Zac adjusted his grip on the handle of the plastic stretcher they were carrying, which was loaded with both the mannequin and all their climbing gear. 'It was a team effort.'

'Yeah…' Mike sounded thoughtful. 'Not just for Doc Donaldson, either. My Shayna was pretty lucky that there happened to be a plastic surgeon in town that day.'

Ben threw a grin over his shoulder. 'Not

the only lucky one, from what I've heard. She stayed with you the night before, didn't she, Zac?'

Zac shook his head. 'Who told you that?'

'Not me,' Bruce said.

'Could have been Debbie,' Mike suggested. 'Or my missus. She put two and two together when Shayna was telling her all about how Doc Donaldson's daughter delivered that foal of yours on the morning of the storm.'

'Not *my* foal,' Zac muttered. 'I'm just baby-sitting till Steve gets back from his mid-life crisis world cruise.'

'He's not coming back, didn't you hear? He's fallen head over heels for someone he met on the cruise and he's planning to sell up and go and live in…where was it, Bruce?'

'Can't remember. Iceland?'

'Nah… I think it was England. Hey, maybe you want to buy the place, Doc.'

'I never own property,' Zac told them.

'Why not?'

'Because I never stay in one place that long. I get itchy feet after a year or so.'

A silence fell amongst the group. They all knew how long he'd been in Cutler's Creek and that meant they were all acknowledging that Zac might not be here for much longer, but no one wanted to say anything aloud, including Zac. He was one of them now. How could he tell them that he had to go somewhere else because he liked being with them too much? That he couldn't allow himself to get too attached to people. Or places. And especially not to any particular person, no matter how profoundly they might have disrupted his world.

It was Mike who finally broke the silence, as they slowed to negotiate a steep part of the track.

'I hope Don will be on his feet well enough for his mum's party. Sounds like it's going to be a right knees-up. My missus is in the Women's Institute and they're doing the catering.'

'I helped shift about a hundred hay bales into the old McDrury barn last weekend,'

Ben added. 'They'd started some of the decorations and it looked awesome.'

'I've heard they've got the best bluegrass band in the South Island, too,' Bruce put in. 'Three fiddles and a caller. People are going to be dancing all night.'

'Mabel will be, that's for sure.'

'I have no idea what to wear,' Bruce said, as their laughter faded. 'Why the heck is it a fifties theme, anyway?'

'I guess that's the era when Mabel was a young woman and out on the town.'

'It's all right for the women to want to dress up but there's nothing for blokes.'

'Oh, I dunno.' Zac was enjoying this distraction.

'Think James Dean or the Fonz. You know, jeans and white T-shirts and a black leather jacket.'

'You're sorted then,' Ben said. 'You've got the jacket.'

'And then there's the gangster look with braces and one of those hats.'

'Reckon I've got a pair of braces somewhere.' Bruce sounded happier. 'In a box of my dad's stuff.'

'She'll have to come back for that, won't she?'

'Who?' But Zac knew exactly who they were talking about and his enjoyment of the conversation evaporated instantly.

'Doc Donaldson's daughter.'

'Nah.' They were back at the parking area now and he helped slide the stretcher onto the back of the ute. 'She didn't bother taking her invitation with her.'

He'd found it that day, on the bedside table in the procedures room, minutes after she'd driven away from Cutler's Creek. And he'd felt guilty about that. He was the one who'd pushed her away, wasn't he? Had he pushed so hard she wasn't even going to consider coming back to her grandmother's birthday party?

'So I don't think she wants to come back,' he added. Not while he was in town, anyway.

Bruce slammed the tailgate of the ute shut.

He slapped his hand on Zac's shoulder as he walked past to get into the driver's seat.

'Maybe you should post it to her,' he said quietly. 'Could be that she left it behind by mistake.'

'Olivia?'

'Yes?' Olivia paused as she walked through the reception area of the Plastic Surgery Institute.

'There's mail for you. A really odd-looking letter.'

'Oh?'

Olivia knew what it was as soon as the embossed envelope was held out to her but she was puzzled about its arrival here at work. During one of her phone conversations with her father in the last few days she had promised to try and come to the party, but who had posted this invitation that she'd left behind at Cutler's Creek Hospital?

Someone who had found it and wanted to make sure she didn't forget the date? *Zac...?*

She didn't open it until she was in the privacy of her consulting room with some time to spare before Peggy Eglington arrived for another appointment to discuss the surgery she was still determined to have.

There was nothing to suggest that it had been Zac who had forwarded the invitation but he was still on her mind as Olivia smiled at the photograph on the front of the card— a woman wearing a polka-dot dress with a circular skirt and cap sleeves, with a big bow on a sweetheart neckline. Quintessential fifties style. The woman was dancing and the skirt was as wide as the smile on her face.

Olivia peered more closely at the image. Was that her grandmother? Kicking up her heels way back when she had been just a young woman? Opening the card confirmed her guess.

Mabel's never stopped dancing!
Come and join us to celebrate her 90th
year of making the most of life.
Classic night of fun
to be held in the McDrury barn
See you there...

It was something on the other side of the card's interior that caught her gaze then. A personal note that had been written beneath a small photograph held in place by a piece of tape.

The note wasn't from Zac. Of course it wasn't, Olivia growled at herself. Why on earth had she thought it might be? Mabel had written it.

I borrowed this from the frame on your dad's bedside table. Maybe you can return it when you come to my party?

It was another picture of Olivia. She'd been a bit older when this one had been taken. Almost eight—just before her world had fallen apart when her father had disappeared from her life. It had been taken at her boarding school and she could remember the moment with absolute clarity, possibly because it was her favourite photo ever and she had exactly the same one in a small heart-shaped silver frame on her own bedside table.

It had been taken in the stables at her

boarding school at the end of a weekend show-jumping event and both Olivia and Koko had been exhausted. The first-place ribbon had been discarded in a puddle of red silk on the straw in the corner of the stable. Koko was also on the straw, half–asleep, and Olivia had curled up between his legs, her arms just reaching around his neck and her cheek pressed against his shoulder. She had filthy jodhpurs, mucky boots and bits of straw in her hair, but to her it was an image of the happiest moment in her life. She only had to look at the photo to remember the warmth of being so close to another living being that she loved so much. The feeling of being in the only place in the world that she wanted to be.

Olivia had tears running down her cheeks as she took the photo from the card and held it in her hand. It wasn't simply the extra evidence of how much her father had always loved her that was her undoing. It was realising that she'd only ever once had that kind of feeling again that she'd had when this photo had been taken, and that had been those moments in Zac's arms—between their lovemaking and finally falling into that dreamless sleep.

It was crazy to miss someone so intensely when she had only known him for such a short time but there it was. Isaac Cameron had rocked her world and it was never going to be the same. She wanted to tell Zac that. Even if he didn't feel the same way and even if he believed he could never get attached to anyone again because of whatever tragedy he'd been through, maybe he should know that he had changed someone else's life for the better.

Maybe it might make a difference if he knew that he was loved. It might even change Zac's life for the better and he deserved that, didn't he?

Olivia dried her eyes and straightened her back, opening her phone to find that voicemail message that had changed her life. The number was still tagged as "unknown". How crazy was that? It felt like she had known Isaac Cameron forever.

It was going to take courage to tap that link and, in that moment of hesitation, Olivia remembered the last time she had been about to do exactly this. She had been going to return the call and tell this stranger what she thought of him. And then she had decided that she would tell her father what she thought of *him* but, in the end, she had chosen to say what she needed to say face to face.

There was even more reason to have this conversation face to face. It would be so much easier to keep the truth hidden when you were on the other end of a phone call. And Olivia really, really needed to know if what was simmering behind all this—somewhere between a longing and a belief—might be true. That you couldn't feel the kind of connection with someone that she had found with Zac if it was totally one-sided.

Simon wasn't going to be too impressed by her leaving town again so soon but, perhaps because Peggy Eglington was the next patient she was due to see, something else was suddenly very clear to Olivia.

This wasn't the place she belonged and it was time she did something about that.

Peggy was in the waiting room as Olivia walked out of the Plastic Surgery Institute after she'd been to talk to Simon.

'I'm so sorry,' she told her client. 'But Simon will be delighted to see you today. I can't stay, I'm afraid. It's a personal thing...'

CHAPTER TEN

No…

It couldn't be. Zac took a second look at the car pulling in to one of the visitors' parks in front of Cutler's Creek Community Hospital. His breath caught as he peered through the window to see the figure climbing out of the driver's seat.

It was definitely Olivia Donaldson. Not that she looked anything like the first time he'd seen her, in that tight skirt and matching jacket. Or the last time, when she'd disappeared wearing hospital scrubs under her coat. Right now, she was wearing jeans and jodhpur-style boots and a warm jumper under an anorak. As if she was quite used to living in a place like this with its hot summers and icy winters.

This was his own fault, Zac realised as

he walked towards the reception area. If he hadn't taken Bruce's advice and forwarded that party invitation, maybe Olivia wouldn't have come back here so soon—and he would have already left the area. This was unsettling, to say the least. Just when things had started to settle down properly and he was feeling completely back in control of his life.

On the other hand, maybe it could be useful. Perhaps Don Donaldson would listen to his daughter and not insist on being back at work when he was only just getting back on his feet. "Light duties" he was calling it but really he should be at home for at least a few more days.

He reached the entrance to Reception just as Olivia was coming in through the front doors and his steps almost faltered as he realised just how unsettling this actually was. It wasn't just that Jill wasn't behind the desk that made it feel as if he and Olivia were the only people on the planet right then. It was a flashback to when she'd come here to tell him about Chloe's foal being born. When

he had still been dazed from what had gone
on between them the night before and when
he'd been aware of a connection that had
made the rest of the world seem irrelevant.
His senses were suddenly heightened to the
point that tiny details were leaping out at
him. How could he have forgotten how incredibly blue her eyes were and surely he
couldn't actually be aware of the scent of her
skin when he wasn't even within touching
distance? And, oh...man...he had completely
blocked the memory of what that smile was
like, hadn't he?

Yep. This was unsettling all right. So why
did it feel good at the same time? As if something at a cellular level was coming alive all
over again?

Olivia's smile was faltering. Because he
wasn't smiling back?

'You're still here,' Olivia said.

'You thought I wouldn't be?' Had she
hoped he wouldn't still be here?

'You said you were planning to leave.'

'I am.' This was better. Talking about future plans was a good way to regain control. 'It's not that easy to find a locum, though. It's always been hard to find anyone who wants to come and live in a one-horse town like Cutler's Creek.'

'I might know someone,' Olivia said. 'Though she might need a refresher course in general medicine and whatever other training is available to work in a rural hospital.'

Zac blinked slowly. '*You?* But… I thought it was the last place you'd want to be.'

'So did I,' Olivia said quietly. 'But I was wrong. I'm starting to think that this might be the place I really belong. And that's thanks to you.'

'Oh?' A prickle of something like premonition made Zac rub the back of his neck. 'How's that?'

'You told me about those letters. And the parcels. I took them back to Auckland with me and…and maybe my mother had some idea what was in them because if I'd opened them and read those books I might have dreamed of coming here a very long time ago. I might never have even gone to medical school and she would have been so disappointed by that. She would have thought I was throwing my life away.'

'What sort of books?'

'Pony stories. Books about Central Otago with the most amazing photographs. And there were stories in Dad's letters. About the people who lived here and what the mountains were like. I could understand why my parents' marriage could never have worked and why my mother might have thought she was protecting me by cutting me off from my dad. But there was so much about how much he missed me and hoped that I would come and visit. So, here I am. For a long visit, I hope…'

Zac was trying to find the words to tell her what good news this was. Because her father and her grandmother would be thrilled. Because it meant that he would be free to leave anytime he wanted. For some reason, however, the words were hard to find and in the slightly awkward silence he became aware of something else. A sound he was very familiar with.

Olivia knew what it was, as well. 'That's the civil defence siren,' she said. 'That means there's an emergency somewhere, doesn't it?'

'Aye.' Zac was reaching for the phone he had in the pocket of his white coat. 'It does.' He activated a rapid-dial number. 'Bruce? What's happening?'

Olivia was watching Zac's face as he made a phone call. She had, in fact, been watching his face very closely from the moment she'd walked in here. He'd felt it, she knew he had. He'd felt that connection between them that might have started as nothing more than a powerful sexual attraction but it had become something far more significant during those intense hours they'd shared since then. Taking it further was a risk, of course. Loving anybody was a risk and maybe Zac wasn't ready to take that risk yet. She could still hear an echo of what he'd said to her that day.

'Sometimes you have to shut yourself off

from something that hurts too much because, if you don't, it can destroy you. It will destroy you.'

Olivia could understand that. He'd loved and lost someone and it would be a huge leap of faith for him to risk doing that again. This was pretty scary for her, as well. She'd come here to offer her heart to him and it was going to be devastating if he didn't want to accept it. He'd said he was still planning to leave Cutler's Creek. And he hadn't even smiled at her.

He certainly wasn't smiling now.

'What...? Oh, no...'

Zac had gone noticeably pale, and for a horrible moment Olivia was reminded of the expression on his face when that plane wreck had caught fire behind them. As if, for a heartbeat, he was somewhere else. Somewhere soul-destroying. From the corner of her eye she saw Jill coming back into Reception, and walking slowly beside her was Don.

'Okay,' Zac said. 'Tell Ben and Tony to

take the ambulance. I'll meet you at the farm...'

'Libby...' Don was smiling at her. 'I didn't tell anyone that you were coming. It's still going to be a surprise for your gran's party tomorrow.' He turned to Zac as he ended his call. 'What's going on?' he asked. 'I heard the siren.'

'Gavin Morris had an accident on his quad bike up in one of his higher paddocks. He might have broken his ankle by the sound of it, getting himself out from under the bike, and he lost his phone so he had to drag himself down to the road to flag down some help.'

'You going to pick him up, then?'

'Yes. And no. There's something else and I don't know where I'll be needed more.'

Olivia could see how still Zac was holding himself. This was something huge, she realised. Something painful...

'He'd taken Jamie out on the bike with him to give Faye a chance to have a sleep while the baby was sleeping.'

'Oh, no...' Don's face creased. 'Jamie's been hurt? He's just a wee lad—two years old now?'

'We don't know if he's hurt,' Zac said. 'He ran off while Gavin was getting out from under the bike and he's vanished. He's somewhere on the side of that mountain and we've got to find him.'

'I'll come, too,' Don said.

'Don't be daft, man. You're in no fit state. What you can do is be here. I might need to send Gavin to you in the ambulance if he needs treatment.' Zac was already heading for the door. 'Maybe you could stay and help your dad, Liv.'

'No.' There was no way Olivia could let Zac walk out that door alone, looking like that. 'I'm coming with you.'

'Yes, go...' Don nodded. 'I can manage here.'

Olivia was shoulder to shoulder with Zac as the doors opened. He turned his head as they walked through them and, this time, as his gaze met hers, that feeling of connection was even stronger. She knew, without a doubt, that Zac wanted her beside him for whatever they were about to face.

He needed her.

There was an unsealed road that led well up into the Morris family's high country farm and a paddock was being used for vehicles to park. Zac's SUV with its magnetic light on the roof was one of the first to arrive, along with the ambulance Ben was driving and Bruce in his police car. Mike and his colleagues from the volunteer fire service arrived a short time later as Zac was assessing Gavin's injury, and then more and more people that Olivia had never met were turning up. One of Cutler's Creek's people was in trouble and the community was gathering to do whatever it could to help. Under Bruce's direction, they were fanning out over the tussock- and rock-covered land, starting to search for a small boy. His helmet had been found, not far from where the quad bike had rolled, but there was no sign of Jamie.

Olivia had helped Zac splint Gavin's ankle.

'It could well be broken given how painful it is,' Zac said. 'But it's not displaced and your limb baselines are all okay for the moment. I'll get Ben to take you in to the hospital and Doc Donaldson can X-ray it for you. You'll need to go to town to get it plastered if it is broken, though.'

'I'm not going anywhere until Jamie gets found. Just give me something for the pain. I've got to help search.'

'Where's Faye?'

'Someone's gone to get her. And the baby.' Gavin covered his face as he groaned. 'What if...? Oh... God...this is unbearable.'

'I know.' Zac gripped his shoulder. 'We'll give you something for the pain and you can stay here for now, in the ambulance. We'll get someone to keep an eye on you but if things get worse, we'll have to take you in to the hospital, okay?'

Gavin scrubbed at his face as he looked up at both Zac and Olivia. 'Can you go and help?' he begged. 'Please… I just need someone to find my son.'

How far could a two-year-old boy go?

The search had been going for an hour. And then another. People were searching in pairs and moving further and further out from where the accident had happened. Olivia was climbing around some big rocks, peering into gaps that could be large enough for a small body to have squeezed into.

'Jamie?' she called. 'Where are you, sweetheart?'

In the silence that followed her call she came to stand beside Zac, following his example to shade her eyes against the lowering sun to look down the slope of this paddock.

'Have you had an update on Gavin?'

'Nothing's changed and his pain's under control. He's got his wife and their new baby in the ambulance with him and they're being well looked after.'

'They must be frantic. I know I would be. That caravan wasn't there before, was it?'

'I think it belongs to the Women's Institute. They'll be providing hot drinks and food for everybody involved in this search. I imagine your gran is down there in the thick of it. She's been running that club forever.'

'She's an amazing woman,' Olivia said. 'I'm really looking forward to getting to know her. And... I can't believe how everybody is here helping. They...they really care, don't they?'

She looked up at Zac and he could see tears shining in her eyes. It was an effort to pull in a breath because of the squeeze he could feel in his own chest.

'Who wouldn't?' he said, a little more sharply than he'd intended. 'This is a two-year-old kid. It's...' He turned away. 'Come on...we've got to keep looking. Let's head for those trees in the gully.'

He strode ahead but Olivia was keeping up with him. She touched his arm. 'What is it, Zac? Tell me...please?'

He walked a few more paces before saying anything. He'd held back from telling her this once before but maybe she needed to know the worst about him. Maybe *that* would keep him safe?

'It was the reason I came here in the first place,' he said. 'A kid of about the same age.'

'He got lost?'

'No. He got beaten up by his stepfather. Drug addict mother didn't even come into ED with him. There was nothing we could do and there was nobody who cared enough to be there with him. Or to hold him while he died.'

Olivia caught his hand in hers. 'What did you do?'

'I held him.'

The squeeze on his hand was sympathetic. 'I can understand why you needed to get away,' she said. 'How heartbreaking that must have been.'

'No, you don't get it.' Zac pulled his hand free from hers. 'That was when I thought I should walk away from medicine completely. Because, after Mia died, I'd taught myself not to care too much. Not to get attached to anything. Or anyone. I thought it was the only way I could keep doing the kind of work I thought I wanted to do for the rest of my life.'

He could still feel the horror of that moment. 'I got to the point where I could hold a dying child and not feel anything but numb and I just wanted to hide. I realised that I had no idea who I was any more and I didn't like the person I'd become. Not caring at all is actually worse than caring too much because it takes any meaning out of life. That's why I came here. To hide. To see if I actually still existed.'

'You *do* care, Zac. You know you do. *I* know you do. It's one of the things I love about you.'

Her words skated past his brain. He knew she was right. He did care again. He could feel the pain of it pressing down on him. He could still take control, though. He knew how to push it away and slam the lid down on the pain that caring so much could bring.

Olivia was slightly ahead of him as they

reached the edge of a gully where the ground dropped sharply. She stopped so abruptly that Zac almost walked into her and he had to catch her shoulders to stop her falling down the steep slope.

And then he looked to see what had made her stop and he froze, as well. The last tree he could see was on such a steep part of the slope that it was growing out at a ninety-degree angle with its canopy hanging over a cliff edge and its twisted, exposed roots clinging to the rocky slope. Curled up in a gap between those huge tree roots was a small boy who was wearing gumboots and a warm coat with a hood. He had his eyes closed and he was so still that Zac could feel his own heart stop for a beat. He could feel it cracking. Was Jamie asleep? Unconscious? Or had the worst happened?

'No...'

Olivia slid out of his grasp and took a step onto the slope. She started to slide instantly and only prevented the momentum of her fall becoming uncontrolled by catching the branches of another small tree.

And something snapped inside Zac as that crack burst wide open.

This was *his* fault. He had persuaded Olivia to be here. By making that phone call in the first place and now by having sent that party invitation. She was here because of him and now she was in danger herself. And there was a small child who was also in danger. Was history trying to repeat itself by creating a combination of the worst moments of Zac's life?

He was sliding down that slope himself before he'd given it any real thought. He had to get to Olivia and make sure she was safe.

'Don't move,' he said, as soon as he could touch her. 'We don't have any idea how high that cliff is. We need to wait for the right equipment.'

'We can't wait,' Olivia said. 'If Jamie wakes up and climbs over those roots, then he's going to fall.'

'I'll go.' Zac still hadn't let go of Olivia. 'This is my fault. I'm going to deal with it.'

'Don't be daft. How on earth is this your fault?'

'You're only here because of me. You said so yourself. I couldn't live with myself if you got hurt. *Please*, Liv…stay here… For me…'

He didn't give her time to argue. Carefully, he let go of both Olivia and the tree that was their anchor to let himself slide down to the next safe point he could see, which was a large rock. Another slide took him close to the tree roots and it was then that he saw Jamie move. The little boy opened his eyes just as Zac reached out to touch him.

'Where's Mummy?' he asked. 'I'm hungry.'

Zac had to swallow past the constriction in his throat to try and make his voice sound normal. 'We're going to go and find Mummy,' he told Jamie. 'Are you okay? Is there anything that hurts?'

Jamie shook his head. He held out his arms. 'Up,' he said. 'My legs are tired.'

Holding Jamie tightly against his body with one arm, Zac started to climb, using his other arm to catch the branches and rocks he needed to keep them safe from sliding towards that cliff. Olivia was waiting to help as they reached the final part of the climb and she took Jamie into her own arms as they finally got back onto safe ground. It was only then that Zac realised he had tears rolling down his face.

He cleared his throat as he hit the speed-dial number on his phone.

'We've found him, Bruce. He's fine. We're heading back...'

His voice cracked on his last word. He looked down at Olivia and Jamie and he had to put his arms around both of them.

'It's okay,' Olivia said softly. 'Everything's going to be okay.' Her sniff suggested that she was crying, as well. 'And it's true that I'm here because of you, Zac, but it's *my* choice to be here and, whatever happens, it's the only place I'm going to want to be.

It's not your fault. You've blamed yourself for too many things that weren't your fault.'

And it was only then that Zac remembered what else Olivia had said.

That she loved him…

He had that strange internal cracking sensation again but this time it was the opposite side of fear and pain. This was joy.

This was love.

The door in that protective barrier was swinging wide open and the pull to step through it was too powerful to resist. This was what being alive was all about. He didn't need to shut feelings like this away. Not when he was with the one person who had brought him back to life. Who was giving him the strength to believe in important things again. Things like life. And love…

Zac needed to hold Olivia even closer. To press his forehead against hers. He still didn't have any words but it felt as though he could communicate anyway. Just for another heartbeat, before they took Jamie back to his family, he wanted to soak in that touch of his skin against hers. That incredible feeling of connection that was so strong you could believe that you would never feel alone again. And that you could cope with anything at all because it would be shared. He wanted to feel love—both given and received—because, in the end, that was all that really mattered, wasn't it?

He knew Olivia didn't want to break that connection, either, because she kept so close to him as they walked back across the paddock. Zac was carrying Jamie who had fallen asleep again in his arms. People were gathering below them and they were all watching. They knew the search was over but they wanted to witness every moment of its joyful conclusion.

'I think we've got the whole of Cutler's Creek watching us,' Zac said.

'I'd better stop hanging on to your arm, then.' Olivia grinned. 'Or the rumours will start.'

'They already have. Everybody knows you stayed with me that night.'

'They don't know that anything happened.'

Zac caught Olivia's gaze and he could see the reflection of exactly what he was acknowledging. That what had happened had been the most amazing thing possible.

'I'm in love with you, Liv. Is that crazy when we hardly know each other?'

'I feel like I've known you forever,' she said. 'And I'm totally in love with you. It feels like I've been looking for you forever.'

'That's it, exactly. For me, too. Even though I didn't know I was looking for you.'

They were almost at the fence of this paddock. People were coming to join them now, needing to be close enough to see for themselves that the fear for one small boy was really over.

Zac slowed his steps so that he could have just another moment of privacy with Olivia.

'And that's how long I want to be with you,' he added. 'Forever.'

'And a day.' She was smiling up at him, tears of joy in her eyes. 'Don't forget about that extra day,' she said. 'There's always an extra day.'

It took a moment before Zac could trust his voice not to crack. 'Absolutely,' he murmured. 'Forever *and* a day.'

EPILOGUE

One year later...

'IT STILL FITS.'

The dress Olivia was wearing was the same one she'd worn to Mabel Donaldson's fifties-themed ninetieth birthday party a year ago. It was a plain dark blue with gores in the skirt that had tiny white polka dots on the blue background and the same spotted fabric peeped out from beneath the heart-shaped neckline. She had left her hair loose but had a silk scarf in a matching blue that she wound around her head and tied in a bow at one side, pulling out enough hair at the front to give herself a boofy fringe, and she was smiling widely as she did a twirl in front of her husband.

'It's not going to fit for much longer. You'll

start showing soon.' The smile they shared acknowledged the secret they'd been keeping for quite a few weeks now. It also acknowledged that life was about to change again in the not-too-distant future but they were more than ready for the coming changes. They couldn't wait, in fact. They'd only waited this long to start a family because Olivia had wanted to get her new postgraduate courses finished and then to settle into her new position as the next generation Dr Donaldson at Cutler's Creek Community Hospital.

Oh, yeah…there'd been the small matter of that glorious summer wedding that they'd held outside with the backdrop of the mountains she now loved so much. The whole town had been invited and the celebration in the community hall afterwards had rivalled Mabel's birthday party as one to remember.

Olivia wanted to do another little twirl to let her skirts billow. She had never dreamed that she would ever be this happy but maybe it took knowing that you were finally living in the place you truly belonged. No, it was more about the people you belonged with than a place, wasn't it? Or one person in particular. She had her soulmate right beside her and she had more family and a whole community around her, as well. It was home and family and forever, all wrapped up together, and it felt just as solid as those mountains she got to admire every day. Blinking back happy tears, she held her hand out to Zac in an invitation to dance with her.

He was wearing faded denim jeans and a close-fitting white T-shirt under a leather jacket. His hair was slicked back, although his curls were already trying to break free of the product and he looked just as gorgeous as he had the first time Olivia had ever set eyes on him. No… More gorgeous, she decided as he caught her in his arms and twirled her around in the kitchen. Then he stopped, pulled her closer and kissed her. Olivia wound her arms around his neck and kissed him back. Somewhere, in the back of her mind, she realised that this was exactly the same place they'd shared their very first kiss. They owned this cottage now and the biggest horse in the world still lived in the paddock they could see from the kitchen window, along with her baby, who was doing his best to grow just as tall.

Finally, they had to break their kiss and come up for air. Reluctantly, Olivia pulled out of Zac's arms, as well.

'I'd better get those sausage rolls out of the oven before that flaky pastry burns to a crisp.' Putting oven gloves on, she pulled out the savoury rolls and wrapped foil and then a towel around the oven tray so they could carry it out to the car. 'Don't forget the tomato sauce,' she reminded Zac.

'Will they have those square cakes again this time? The pink ones with the coconut on the outside?'

'Lamingtons? Of course. It has to be a classic Kiwi supper.' Olivia smiled. 'I'm so glad Gran decided to have another fifties party this year. It was all a bit of a blur last time, what with so much happening in such a short space of time. And it was all so new for me.'

'You'll get used to it. Mabel told me the other day that she was going to have this party again every year from now on,' Zac told her. 'That every year after ninety was a bonus that needs celebrating and you can't beat the fifties for a party.'

'At least this year Dad will be well enough to dance.'

'He'll be showing us all up on the dance floor, from what I've heard.'

'I know. He and Jill have been going to rock 'n' roll dance classes for months now.'

'Do you think there's something going on there?'

'I hope so.'

'Maybe they'll announce something at the party tonight.'

'Maybe *we* should announce something.'

They shared another smile. 'Maybe we should.'

It was time that Mabel Donaldson stopped dancing.

Just long enough to catch her breath, mind

you. And to find where she'd left her glass of champagne.

She paused for a moment beside a stack of hay bales and looked around her party. The music was loud and almost everyone was still on the dance floor. She could see Don and that lovely Jill, who was about to take over Mabel's presidency of the Women's Institute. My word, those two could dance now. And Don looked so happy. Happier than he had ever looked. Mabel knew that had a lot to do with his daughter coming back into his life. Into all their lives.

Including that lovely young man Isaac Cameron, who was not only going to stay in Cutler's Creek forever but was also now part of her very own family. Married to her gorgeous granddaughter. They were dancing, too, and they looked for all the world as if they were on their very own dance floor. Staring into each other's eyes as if they were even more in love than ever.

Last year's birthday, when she'd turned ninety, had been very special, of course. The surprise that Olivia had come back in time for her party had been the best gift possible. But this year's surprise—learning that she would be meeting her first great-grandchild in about six months' time—well…could life get any better?

Now…where *had* she left that glass of champagne?

* * * * *

LET'S TALK
Romance

For exclusive extracts, competitions
and special offers, find us online:

f facebook.com/millsandboon

⊙ @millsandboonuk

𝕏 @millsandboon

Or get in touch on 0844 844 1351*

For all the latest titles coming soon,
visit millsandboon.co.uk/nextmonth

*Calls cost 7p per minute plus your phone company's price per
minute access charge

Want even more
ROMANCE?

Join our bookclub today!